Michael Myers Shoemaker

The Kingdom of the White Woman

Michael Myers Shoemaker

The Kingdom of the White Woman

ISBN/EAN: 9783337240691

Printed in Europe, USA, Canada, Australia, Japan

Cover: Foto ©Andreas Hilbeck / pixelio.de

More available books at **www.hansebooks.com**

THE KINGDOM OF THE "WHITE WOMAN"

A SKETCH

M M Shoemaker

CINCINNATI
ROBERT CLARKE & CO
1894

PREFACE.

These notes are the record of a winter in Mexico, at a time when the first waves of a second and greater conquest were beginning to break on her shores. When we in the North were awakening to the fact that just to the southward slept in an enchanted kingdom, not one maiden but a whole nation, and that the time had come to awaken them from a sleep of 300 years—so we turned our faces southward, not in battle array, not in glittering hosts, and carrying neither cross nor crescent, but in small groups at first, who, as we entered the kingdom, felt that the place was haunted, and stole wonderingly on in silence. Then more and more followed, pushing wider and wider the long-forgotten portals, until now through each and all rolls a "flood tide" that in the name of peace and progress will rush onward until its mighty waters will submerge the sea of Mexico into the ocean of a "greater America."

(3)

CONTENTS.

Contents.

KINGDOM OF THE "WHITE WOMAN."

CHAPTER I.

On board the S. S. "City of Vera Cruz." In roadstead off the port of Pergresso, Yucatan; the season, midwinter.

A TROPICAL sun sends its rays downward so strong and so direct that an awning is necessary, and one's disposition to do any thing is at its lowest ebb. Around about us are scattered the members of a French opera troupe, *en route* to charm the inhabitants of the one-time kingdom of Montezuma. Here is the *prima donna*, tall and stately, with glorious dark eyes. She seems really a lady. The rest are, to say the least, an odd lot. We have been

(9)

almost a week on board with them, and
have not as yet been able to establish the
different relationships. However, we probably know as much about it as they do
themselves, and it is needless to say, do
not tell all we know. Here comes the contralto, a big, heavy woman, who evidently
believes that variety is life's spice, as one
never sees her with the same man twice,
except it be that cadaverous priest, with
whom she is now walking and whom she
persists in tormenting. The poor man tries
to ignore her and bury his nose in his
breviary, but she is not of the sort to be
ignored. As they cross that patch of sunlight near the funnel, I see her give his old
greasy *soutane* such a jerk that his breviary
nearly flies into the sea, and he crosses
himself devoutly. Now she snatches his
arm, and church and opera pass around
the ship in stately procession, much to the

amusement of the latter, as well as the rest of us.

Our attention is suddenly diverted from the life of the ship to the life of the ocean that spreads around us in oily waves. Those engaged in the business of shark fishing find that they have succeeded at last, and are tugging hand over hand, endeavoring to handle their prize. Leaning over the rail, I recoil with a shudder as I find myself looking straight down the throat of one of those monsters of the deep—a mouth nearly half a yard across holds row after row of savage looking teeth, back of which cold, cruel, and most malignant looking eyes stare straight into mine. To my mind Nature holds nothing so horribly cruel in expression as the eye of a shark. This is a monster some fourteen feet long. The men have almost gotten him over on the deck when the chain parts and he vanishes, carrying as a memento of his curiosity an iron hook in his jaws about a foot long. It will soon turn him into food for the hundreds of others that fill the sea around us. It really would seem to be a fact they do not attack negroes. At least here, where we see that the waters abound with the monsters, the blacks do not hesitate to plunge in, appearing to be utterly devoid of fear. Just over yonder, man and monster actually appear to be engaged in a game of water polo.

CHAPTER II.

WE have been anchored for two days off this port of Merida waiting for the winds and waves to subside. These steamships being subsidized by the Mexican government to carry the mails, do not dare leave without them, so we roll at anchor for forty-eight hours waiting the pleasure of that apparently dead town. The sun shines from a cloudless sky, but the wind and waves keep up a dolorous moaning. Captain Van Sice (poor man, he went down with this same ship some two years later) says that it is the "tail of a norther" and will end soon. It does so (*after two days*), then the natives come off in clumsy lighters and in a few hours we are again under full steam westward. Frontrara is passed in like manner, and to-morrow should find us landed at Vera Cruz. To-night the ocean sleeps peacefully and the moon will rise toward eleven o'clock (over quiet waters). We have gathered on deck to hear the opera troupe rehearse "Mignon," and when they finish the purser produces his accordion and we assist him in returning the compliment. It is needless to say that "The Blue Bahamas," and one or two other familiar airs are rendered more or less perfectly. Rarely have we heard an accordion played so well. There is music in it as he swings it around his head— music so inspiring that French, English, and Americans, officers and crew, are soon tripping the light fantastic, with the exception of the priest who has locked himself in his state-room to escape the embraces of the contralto. Heavens! he laughs best who laughs last. Having missed the holy father, she insists upon dancing with me. What a waltz it is! I have had many dances in many climes but never any thing equal to this. Released at last I lean panting against the wheel-house, and gaze eastward to where the reddening of the sky tells of the coming moon. The waters of the gulf spread darkly around us like a vast black mirror, over which the queen of night casts a long river of light, and which ever and anon heaves slowly as though the giant spirit of the ocean were deep in slumber—but the coming of the moon disturbs him. The waters are deeply troubled, and rise and fall uneasily in swirls and whirlpools. Now the wind begins its moaning, grows stronger and stronger, swifter and swifter, until it howls through the rigging like mad. In less than twenty minutes the norther is upon us, and all night long we pitch and toss upon a tempestuous ocean.

CHAPTER III.

GOOD FRIDAY, 1879.

THE hours of the night are filled with the sound of moaning winds and dashing waves. Morning brings us no comfort. I find on reaching the deck that the storm still rages and every thing is shrouded in mist. We are at anchor between the castle of San Juan d' Ulloa and the city of the True Cross, so they say, but we seem to be anchored in cloudland.

Suddenly the mist separates, and through the rift, against the blue sky, comes the first glimpse of the peak of Orizaba,* a perfect cone of snow, sparkling twenty thousand feet above us. The rift grows wider as

*" Mountain of the Star."

the rising sun sends more power into its
rays. Shortly there appear the gray rocks;
then the light green tops of the higher
mountain trees, followed by the dark, glistening foliage of the tropics on the lower
hills; then, as with a last effort, the mist
is banished completely, like the falling of
a curtain, the entire panorama spreads
before us. Long dunes stretch from the
base of the mountains in waves of sand,
until they seem about to overwhelm the
sleeping city of Vera Cruz, lying over there
all pink and green and white in the early
sunlight. Silence most intense, save for
the sound of the dancing waters of the
gulf, reigns over all. The view is most
beautiful, yet it is intensely melancholy,
for all is so white and hot and desolate,
while the moaning of the wind seems with
the waves to be chanting a solemn requiem
over this city of the True Cross,—this spot

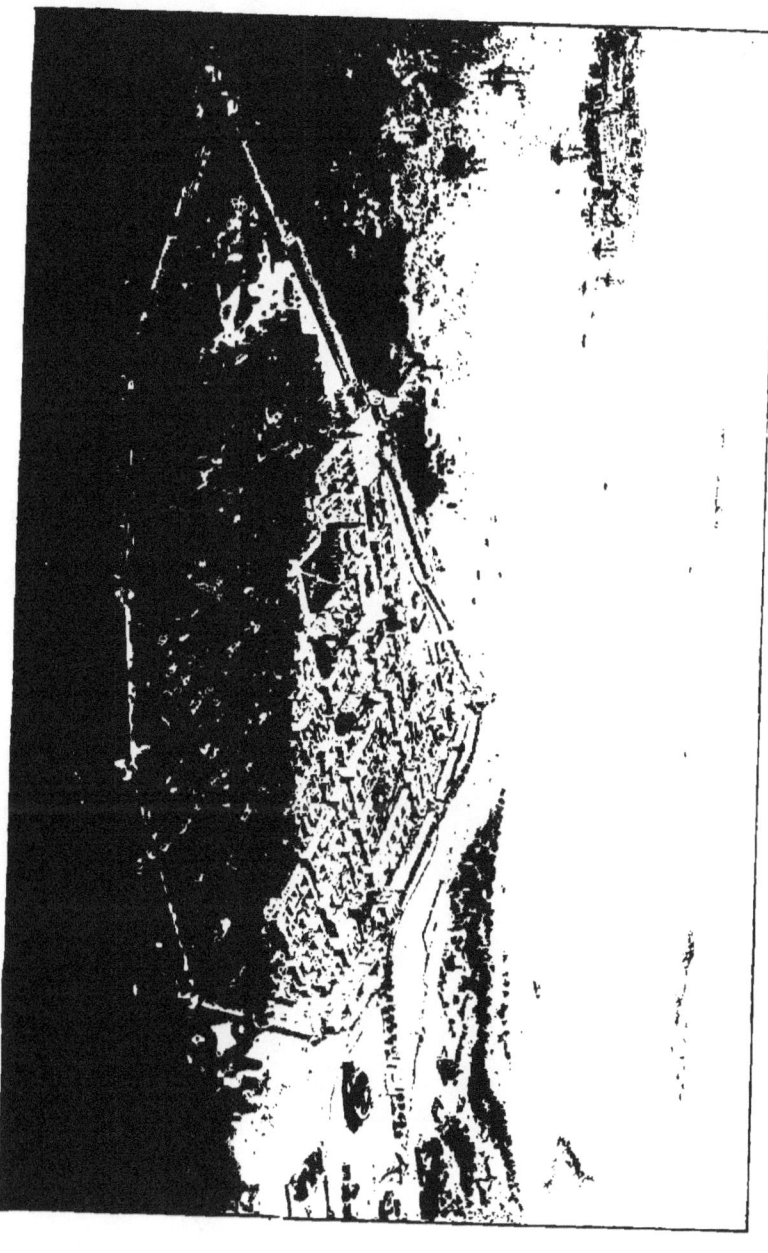

VERA CRUZ.

where Cortez first set foot in the ancient kingdom of Montezuma.

There is no harbor here nor anywhere else on this coast, only an open roadstead, on one side of which rises the fortress of San Juan d' Ulloa, while on the other stretches the low-lying Terra Caliente, with the city of Vera Cruz encircled by its perfect .walls in the middle foreground. The houses are truly Spanish with their flat roofs and gayly-colored walls. Up one street we catch a glimpse of the plaza and cathedral, around which, the only signs of life are the vultures. To the very gates of the city the sand has blown in great hills, and we do not see what is to prevent a fate like that of Pompeii overwhelming all.

It is hard work enjoying all this when

we are forced to cling to the railing and
rigging, the ship rocking constantly beneath
us, while the wind never ceases. A howling
storm, with clouds and darkness, thunder
and lightning, has something awe inspiring
about it, but to me nothing is more lonely
than a brilliant sunny day, with the wind
blowing steadily and moaning as only such
winds can moan; and when is added to
this a silent fortress, a sleeping or apparently deserted city, over which great clouds
of sand are drifting, and beyond which the
desert stretches away to the mountains—
one has reached the acme of desolation.
Nature would be lonely here under all
circumstances, but she is never at any time
or place desolate, unless man has left his
track across her face, and when these tracks
are in the form of a city and fortress, whose
life and usefulness are long over past, the
desolation is intense.

CHAPTER IV.

SAN JUAN D'ULLOA.

"TWENTY years in the dungeons of San Juan d' Ulloa." Such was the sentence pronounced not long since upon a murderer in northern Mexico. Twenty years! He will not live three. The dungeons of this old fortress are in the solid rock, much lower than the waters of the ocean, whose rising tides drive the rats and vermin in upon those buried alive there. Ooze and slime trickle down walls that are foul with disease. Yellow fever and small-pox are forever rampant. Escape from the fortress is impossible. You are literally "between the devil and the deep sea." The former in the shape of the pestilence, and the latter in the great depths of the water and the myriads of sharks ;—so abandon your hopes if once you enter this castle of San Juan d' Ulloa. Russia holds no prison more terrible. As we stand on our deck regarding its storm-washed walls we are startled by a wailing cry and the sight of two poor white hands extended toward us from one of the iron-barred casemates, behind which a half-starved face looks out imploringly. It is too much, and we rush across the deck, down the companion-way, and into the first boat that is to venture shoreward, leaving San Juan d' Ulloa to her silence and her waves.

CHAPTER V.

VERA CRUZ.

A S the landing is dangerous we decide to drift for half an hour, when finally it appears safe to venture. Even then "Madam," the contralto, gets soaked by a high breaker just as she makes a rush for the portal, and the last we see of her she is vanishing down a long street in any thing but a good humor, while she carries her pet parrot by the tail. With it all, she was a jolly soul, and whether she meets priest or pagan will go singing through life's pathway. Sunshine be with her, for she has afforded us many a hearty laugh.

Are these black-robed priests, with shovel-shaped hats, who advance to meet us, from the *Barber of Seville*, or is that big-nosed one a demon from *Hendrick Hudson's crew?* They bow their heads in solemn silence, as though they were one or both, and the one of the big nose offers us a drink of something white and ill-smelling. We know it is only pulque, but they seem to watch us with a sinister sidelong glance, wondering whether we will drink. If we did would we hear the ghostly "ha, ha," "ha, ha," as we sink into slumber, like those silent figures down that long quiet street yonder? Each and all of us decline to try the experiment, and moving onward enter the portals of this first city of the Conquest.

CHAPTER VI.

"I S this all you have for dinner?" "Si,
Señor." "Then serve it over again."
The waiter stares for a moment and, departing, soon returns with the first course
of the dinner which we have already tried
and found wanting in quantity, hence our
party seated in the cool, dark dining
room have decided, with much laughter,
to go through the menu again, which they
do and are not over fed with the double
dinner.

The brilliant tropical sun streams in
at the open door and through the Vene-
tian blinds in long rays of slanting light,
which penetrating into the cracks and corners, drive the roaches and spiders deeper

into their dens of dirt. There is never any thing clean in Vera Cruz, and you soon cease to wonder that yellow fever has an eternal abiding place here. Out in the square the dogs and vultures quarrel unceasingly over the accumulated piles of filth. Ever and anon the vultures arising in countless numbers, slowly circle above you, settling at last all over the domes of the old cathedral, only to be driven away by the discordant clangor of her cracked bells. Through the still air comes the musical gurgling note of the " Clarine." Here and there and every-where sleeping beggars ' lie around in sunshine and shadow, looking more like bundles of filthy rags than ' any thing human. Indeed, you would take them for such until you become aware of a pair of sinister eyes closely regarding you from one end of said bundle, and which tell you plainly that were it night they would take all you have, even to your life, provided they could stab you from behind; but as it is day they will try to filch or beg your purse. Down on the ground floor of the house the beggars and animals are stalled together, while from the center of the court stench from the dung heap fairly stifles one as he climbs the greasy stone stairway, past the second floor, the abode of the proprietor and his help, to the grand *étage*, where as in all Mexican houses, the better living rooms are to be found.

Dinner being over, we adjourn to the house-top for a view of this ancient town stretching beneath us, and surrounded by the original walls still as perfect as when the builders left them three centuries ago. Across the bay rises the fortress of San Juan d'Ulloa. How can such an ulcer

seem so beautiful? Around it and away
into the hazy distance stretches the sparkling ocean—asleep now after the terrible
norther that has kept all ships from landing passengers or cargo for two days
past. During such storms the waves break
clear over the walls of the city, and if
you are unfortunate enough to anchor as
one commences, there you must abide
until it is over, though but a few hundred
yards from the pier and the gate of the
city. Not a sign of life will be visible
though the wind blows for a month, until you begin to believe that what the
fever has spared the winds have buried
deep in the shifting sands. Sometimes
the sun pours its flood of golden light
downward during the entire storm; then
the sight of those great green waves
breaking over the brilliantly painted town
is beautiful in the extreme. Away on the

other side stretch the low dunes of the coast, while the dark foliage of the Terra Caliente rises gradually, terrace on terrace, until in the distance the gigantic walls of the great table-land of Mexico appear to bar the way to all further progress; while over all the snowy cone of Orizaba glitters like a diadem. Only when the winds have moaned themselves to sleep will the gates of the town open and the drowsy gens-d'armes appear yawning on the quay. I have no doubt that they are forced to awaken even then and are indignant that these American ships will not permit them to postpone all things until the arrival of that Spaniards' day of reckoning— "Mañana" (to-morrow).

At least, judging by the sullen looks with which they greeted us this morning, I think they would willingly have consigned us to a fate like unto that which was meted out to three Englishmen. With the usual daring recklessness of their race, they entered into a wager (not long since) that they could swim from the castle to the pier. Only one accomplished it. Nothing save shrieks, wildly tossing arms, and a shadow of blood on the water, told of the fate of the others.

Before leaving the ship we were shown the jawbones of a shark that had been captured in these waters by the sailors during the last voyage. They were so enormous, that when opened they could be passed over a man's shoulders.

'

' CHAPTER VII.

W AS yellow fever known to the Indians, or is it only a result of the
" higher civilization" introduced with the
advent of Spain and the bearers of the
" One. True Cross?" We are blessed with
a consul here who seems proof against it.
Some time since, on hearing that his suc-
cessor had arrived on one of the ships, he
went out to greet him, and assured him that
he would not be able to live in the place—
would die of yellow fever before the year
was out. The new-comer was so terribly
frightened that he did die of the disease
before he had time to land; so Mr. G.
staid on and on, until old age, not fever,
called the time on him. A lazier man I
never saw. Going in one morning, at about

eleven o'clock, I find himself, wife, and some of his family playing on violins and violoncellos, and dressed in as little as possible. What there is of it has certainly been slept in. At any rate, it is of a description more suited for bed than the reception room.

We are favored with a call from him later, and pressed to attend a ball that is to come off that night. "But we are not invited, and you say it is private; then, again, we leave at midnight, and are in our traveling clothes."

"None of these reasons will hold good here," was the answer. "They will be glad to see you, and your clothes are all right for Vera Cruz."

So we go, and at the very entrance, under a bower of palms, are greeted by the host and hostess faultlessly appareled in full evening dress. However, we can not run

away now, so we sail boldly forward. I
hitch at my collar in a vain endeavor to hide
its soaked appearance, consequent on the
sea bath received in landing, while the ladies
with one shake put themselves in perfect
condition for any thing. It takes an American woman to do that. The ball is beautiful. These Mexican houses are all built
around open courts, and here the moon
shines down where the magnolia leaves glis-
ten and stately palms wave softly, keeping
time to the music of the fountains, while the
band of musicians in the marble arcade
above are playing a national melody on soft-
toned mandolins. As we enter, there appears to be a grand promenade in progress,
but shortly the couples interchange and pass
through some of the figures of our lanciers,
varied now and then by a slowly drifting
waltz. It is the famous "Danza," and is
charming. We have to thank these people

of Vera Cruz for a delightful entrance into
their country. The ball is a bit of the pro-
verbial hospitality of old Spain; and where
will you meet with its equal? We find it
hard to leave, and it is close on to midnight
before our party descend and walk through
the silent streets to where the train awaits
to carry us to the capital.

CHAPTER VIII.

MEXICO possesses but one railroad (1879), and therefore its managers do very much as they please, and travelers suffer in consequence. Each end of the train carries a van full of soldiers, who to me appear much more disposed to rob than to protect. Still, as they are well paid, for Mexico, and we are armed, we shall probably get through in safety, though this part of the world is more celebrated for its brigandage than all the rest put together. It was a common thing, in the old days of the stage, to be stopped fifteen or twenty times. Even after you had entered the gates of the City of Mexico you were not safe, and were sure to arrive with nothing save what nature gave you. So certain was this to be the case that your friends in the town always sent word that they would meet you at the Barrièr with papers, wherewith you might, in a measure, clothe yourself. But we hope for better luck, as we roll out of the Vera Cruz station and settle down for a few hours sleep while crossing the Terra Caliente (Hot-land). The cars are of the common English type, and we snatch a few hours of wretched sleep as best we may, half sitting, half lying, and wholly uncomfortable. It does not seem an hour since starting, when we are awakened by a clap of thunder and a dash of rain against the windows. What a changed world is before us! Gone is the sleepy ocean, the yellow, desolate sand dunes, and the hot, enervating air of the torrid zone. Now all is fresh and strong, full of life and vigor, and the towering mountains are around us every-where. Our train rushes through gorges and over bridges spanning roaring torrents. At Cordova we alight in the midst of coffee plantations, beds of flaming tropical flowers, and hosts of flying parrots. The Cordilleras have closed in around us, and white-headed Orizaba seems a near neighbor.

CHAPTER IX.

NOTWITHSTANDING our knowledge of the character of these people, we decided (two of us) to take the stage overland from Cordova to Orizaba, some sixteen miles, and there board the train for the capital. I think our safe transit was due to the fact that no one had dared attempt this route for years; hence we were not expected.

Cordova is more tropical than Orizaba, being some hundreds of feet further down the mountains. As we sit in her little hotel, eating our breakfast and waiting for the stage to start, long avenues of the coffee plant stretch away before us. Resembling the willow, with the berry growing close to the stem and under the leaves, it forms a

thick hedge on either side of the way.
Flaming Hibiscus and poppies are every-
where, while overhead the orange blossoms
fill the air with their dreamy fragrance, and
fall now and then in snowy showers. At
the far end of a tropical street, silent and
deserted as are all tropical streets the moment the sun touches them, rise the green
ridges of the lower mountains, while high
above soars the grand cone of Orizaba.
That old mountain is the guardian of this
section of the land. You never lose sight
of it until you enter the valley of the capital.

As we drive away, parrots chatter at us
from the house-tops and trees. That we do
not run over some of these sleeping figures
in the streets is a miracle. They do not
move an inch. Look out there! A fraction
more and that man's head would have been
gone. He shows no consciousness of his
danger, but simply hugs tighter his ragged

serape, and draws down more closely the
greasy sombrero, composing himself to a
sleep that will last all day, broken only by
his animal sense of hunger; even that will
not keep him awake long. But, when night
comes he will rise, and with the swift, silent
movement of our northern Indian, skulk
around for hours. Then it will behoove
you, if you meet him in the moonlight or
darkness, to be well on your guard, for he
does not love you. He would take great
delight in running that long murderous-
looking stiletto between your ribs—that
would be a pleasure not to be deferred,
even until *mañana*.

This ride is one long to be remembered, for many reasons. The wagon has
no springs, and if there has ever been a
road it has been abandoned. I think our
driver makes it a point to drive over every

enormous bowlder on the mountains. The horses can climb like cats, and as long as the harness and wagon hold together, and we manage to stay in the latter, we are bound to get on ; but there is no chance for conversation, nor can we admire much of the scenery. When the horses halt at noon, we are surrounded by a lot of as villainous-looking rascals as the world holds, and it dawns upon us that perhaps we may be robbed, if not murdered. However, I think either the " professionals " in these hills are away, or they are too much astounded at our impudence in coming to act in the matter. In the end we rush onward, leaving them still gaping and scarcely sufficiently awake to realize what had happened.

After an hour's more torture, we roll into Orizaba, just as the train which contains a woman from Hoosierdom draws up.

Her face expresses strong disappointment at our safe arrival, as she has confidently predicted both robbery and murder.

Of the scenery on the ride we have not the smallest recollection, and we would not take it again to see the mountains of Eden.

CHAPTER X.

WHILE in Cordova some very amus-
ing things happened. If you know
who the ladies were that accompanied me
on my last tour, you have my full permis-
sion to question them thereon.

At Orizaba, climate, foliage, and flowers
are all as in our own latitude in May.
From there onward we mount, and twist,
and turn, until with an extra snort the
great double-ended engine, having accomplished its task, pauses at Boca del Monte,
the end of as daring a piece of railway
engineering as the world holds except,
perhaps, the "Meigs R'y," in Chili.
During the ascent the traveler feasts his

eyes upon a most marvelous panorama. Leaving Orizaba he might fancy that the train is rushing through the gorges of our Alleghenies—the same fresh air and rushing waters, the same foliage. Only now and then, by a glimpse of the snow masses of the upper mountains, he sees that here nature is cast in a grander mold. The quaint town of " Maltrata" is passed, and at Esperanze on the great upper Table-Land we are served with fruits and coffee for breakfast, all the while submitting to a close inspection from a wretched, thieving looking lot of people, who are only prevented by the soldiers from laying violent hands on the " heretics." One does not feel entirely safe until the guard locks the train doors, and it draws slowly out on what proves to be a long, dusty ride to Pueblo. Still the sights and sounds are so strange and foreign that it is not an uninteresting day. Behind us rises the wall of mountains sweeping away in dignified magnificence east and west, and forming the rim of this great flat basin over which we are moving. As level and limitless as our own western plains, it stretches away to the northward, desolate and devoid of life or movement, save for some majestic moving pillars of dust and some millions of cacti, with here and there a skulking dog and slouching Mexican, moving off with gaits so near alike that were it not for the upright position of the latter it would be difficult to distinguish between them. It is indeed impossible to do so at a distance, and as you approach, both man and beast settle into watchful silence; the sombrero of the former is slouched more and more over his evil face, while the wolf-like head of the latter is buried in his shaggy hair.

CHAPTER XI.

THIS people have certainly reduced highway robbery to a science. Not long since there pulled out of the station of the capital a train loaded with silver for exportation. It was carefully inspected before starting and carefully guarded during the journey; yet on the arrival at Vera Cruz, one car had been completely emptied of its valuable cargo, leaving no trace of where it occurred, though the "how" was plainly to be seen. One of the rogues had attached himself to the bottom of the car, and with the aid of a small saw effected an entrance. You must understand that these trains at that time (1879) moved slowly—three hundred and forty miles in eighteen hours—to believe that this could be done, as done it was. Once inside, the rest was simple enough. He had only to drop the bags through the hole at certain previously agreed upon points, where they were quickly spirited away, and not one dollar ever recovered. All of which illustrates the old adage, "If a thing is worth doing at all, it is worth doing well." As the millions of " the people" are a great band of thieves, even the expert Adams Express Company could not have recovered the vanished silver.

"Well, old man, never mind the robbers. Just look at this." And the speaker holds up a superb pineapple, whose fragrance fills the air. It is so perfectly ripe that we pull it to pieces by sections, finding even the core tender and juicy, and is so different from the leathery stuff offered us under the name at home that no one would know it as

the same fruit. With it is sold that strange
production of nature called "cherry moya,"
about the size of an orange, with a rough,
dark green rind, which, on being cut open,
displays a soft, white paste, tasting like va-
nilla cream. They say that nothing save
water must be taken with it; wine or liquor
of any kind producing distress and sometimes serious illness. Here is also the
granadita, a yellow gourd, whose contents
look like tapioca; the sappodilla, potato-
like on the outside, pink inside, and tasting
like a rotten apple. On the whole, aside
from the pines and oranges, I do not care
for Mexican fruits. Most of them are an
acquired taste, and I hear a man's voice
outside, saying, " Well, I would give all of
these for one northern pear. Just live here
as long as I have, and you will become thoroughly nauseated with the very smell of a sappodilla." All of which I can readily believe.

CHAPTER XII.

OUR train rolls onward, and the glare and the heat are oppressive. This plateau must, at some period in the world's history, have been the basin of a vast lake. Now it is used for the cultivation of the cactus plant, from which comes the national drink, "pulque," a liquid looking like skimmed milk and intoxicating in its effects. Yet it is simply the fermented juice of the cactus, and is drawn from that plant by means of a long copper tube, shaped like a gourd, one end of which is driven into the stalk of the plant, while a native, holding the other between his lips, sucks the liquid into the tube. Here, there, and every-where you see these serape-draped and sombrero-crowned figures standing silently at this work. The liquor is carried in pig-skins all over the land, and I know of no stranger sight than a long train of flat cars loaded with these skins full to bursting. Every movement makes them quiver with apparent life.' As the train pauses now and then, natives come up, and untying a leg or neck, take long draughts therefrom. All through the towns and cities pulque shops take the place of the bar-rooms of our country, and the sour smell coming from them is most disgusting.

Our train moves at a jog trot, and every now and then pulls up alongside of one pulque-ladened, the smell from which forces us to close the carriage windows. After many hours of heat and dust, we finally halt at Appizaccio, the junction for Pueblo de los Angelos, whither we are bound, for Pueblo is three

centuries old, and possesses the most beautiful cathedral in all the land. As we await the starting of the train, we are treated to a sight of one of the most superb specimens of mankind that it has ever been our good fortune to look upon. Fully six and one-half feet in height, and splendidly proportioned, he is garbed in closely-fitting black; down the seams of his trousers run broad bands of silver embroidery, while his feet are incased in English riding shoes, with spurs attached. The short jacket is heavily embroidered with silver, and from beneath a jeweled and embroidered sombrero gaze a pair of wondrous black eyes, giving life to a face perfect in every line, and set off by waving curls. He knows he is handsome, and I am obliged to hustle the ladies into the car or run the risk of being utterly deserted. I am strongly under the impres-

sion that he is the great matadore, Manzan-
tin, who has been brought over from Spain,
and will receive $15,000 for three perform-
ances in the ring at Pueblo and the City of
Mexico.

CHAPTER XIII.

THE quaint old town of "Pueblo de los Angelos" went to sleep centuries ago. Quiet reigns in her streets and squares, under her shady arcades, and within the solemn silence of her beautiful cathedral, whose walls are built of precious marbles and onyx, and adorned with many jewels. As they catch the light of the sun through the painted windows they glow and quiver with renewed life, and then go to sleep once more, as though it were useless to rebel against the established order of things. The great orange trees in the square are laden with fruit and snowy with blossoms, whose fragrance fairly overpowers one. Perhaps it is the cause of the general sleepy

condition of place and people. At any rate,
between sunshine and perfume, we find ourselves soon seated where the shadows are
thickest, where the quiet is most intense,
and where we are lulled ere long into slumber by the splashing fountains. This is
what we came for, so why go any farther.
We will awaken later, and stroll out by that
jaloused window, behind which a fan and
dark eyes have been beckoning to and
watching us for an hour. We are told that
the view is superb from the roof of the
church, but sunset is a better time for that;
so let us slumber on until then, lulled by
the falling waters, soothed by the gurgling
music of the clarines.

The altitude of this city is over seven
thousand feet, and when one tries to climb
to the cathedral towers one fully realizes
the fact. Still the panorama unfolded be-

fore them repays all fatigue and shortness of breath.

In the center of a green valley, full of running streams and glistening lakes, stands this City of the Angels, while off in the distance rises the pyramid of Cholula. In the days of the Aztecs it was crowned by a temple to the God of the Air, while around the base spread a city old before the days of Montezuma, and as sacred to her people as is Mecca or Benares to the millions of the old world. There occurred that terrible retribution taken by Cortez for the butchering of his soldiers; and now, even from here, one can see the white arms of the cross gleaming from the spot where once stood the shrine of the heathens. Beyond it rises the great mountain of Popocatapetl like a vast cone of sugar against the deep blue of the sky, while in the encircling chain the peaks of Ixtaccihuatl and Molenki

stand forth most prominently. It is said
that in the days of old, when in the North
Gitche Manito, the mighty, descended and
called the nations together, here in this
peaceful land Popocatapetl and his wife
Ixtaccihuatl lived harmoniously, he smok-
ing occasionally a pipe of peace and so-
ciability with their neighbor, Bachelor Molenki.   But Ixtaccihuatl could not forego
the desire of her sex, and one day, when
Popocatapetl was slumbering, carried on a
flirtation with Molenki.   Popocatapetl awakening suddenly, saw the entire performance, and great was his indignation.
Fiercely waxed the battle.   Each belched
forth great volumes of flame and smoke,
while Ixtaccihuatl looked placidly on as
though entirely innocent.   Hoary headed
Orizaba watched the state of affairs from
afar with great disapproval, yet the etiquette
of the mountains would not permit him to

interfere until things reached such a point that the world was threatened with destruction. Then he quietly sent "Ahousca" (that purple mountain yonder, shaped like a hog's back, which, by the way, is the meaning of the name) to inform the powers that control even such things as volcanos. (I should like to say just here that I have spelled the names of these mountains as they are pronounced.)

At any rate, it was noticed that a sudden calm came over each and all; that Ixtaccihuatl retired unto herself, and drawing a vast winding sheet over her recumbent form sank into a slumber uninterrupted to this day, that Popocatapetl grumbled no more, and Molinki became forever silent, and thus they stand. You can plainly see the sleeping form of the wife under her mantle of snow, while husband and lover having drawn on their night-caps slumber on forever. The .

moon is rising .slowly and grandly over the sleeping "White Woman" as we descend from the tower, and one can almost fancy that one sees her move; but if so it is only to compose herself to a more profound slumber. Others believe that Ixtaccihuatl is the sleeping Montezuma, and that some day he will arise, and driving the strangers from his kingdom, seize his own once more. To this day you will see on many house-tops strange groups of figures intently gazing toward his sleeping form, watching and waiting for his coming.

CHAPTER XIV.

THE Pyramid of Cholula, which rises from the plain some three miles from Pueblo, at first sight, might be taken for one of those Indian .mounds so often to be found in our own land. Though the sides of its base are twice the length of those of the Great Pyramid of Cheops, it is only about one-third as high as the .Egyptian structure. The centuries that have rolled by since Cortez looked first upon it have clothed all with a thick jungle of tropical foliage, and it is only here and there the traveler can discern the original brick-work used in the construction. The ancient road-way still winds around to its summit, where now the little white church holds aloft the emblem of Christianity (and from which the altar to the God of the Air has vanished long ago). One could almost wish that the ruins of the heathen temple had been allowed to remain; but not a bit of the sacrificial stone, and no capital or pillar can be found either here or in the valley where once stood the city with its streets and squares—nothing here, save the little white chapel; nothing below, save a few wretched huts and a handful of more wretched people, whose only occupation seems to be sleeping and the drawing of pulque. No thoughts of daring deeds or human sacrifice with them; no high festivals to either the Nazarene or to the God of the Air, and I doubt if you questioned them whether they would know the difference between the two.

As we gaze upon the land spread out before us, one of those sudden tropical

storms comes on, preceded by a most
fantastic chasing of light and shade across
the valley and by the formation and stately
progress of three gigantic "dust spouts"
that move swiftly from place to place.
They are dangerous looking things, and I
notice men and beasts fleeing from their
pathway. A sudden darkening of the
heavens, followed by a down-pour of rain
wipes them out, and for awhile seems to
have wiped out every thing else. From
our shelter we can not see a yard, so
tremendous is the deluge. It passes as
suddenly as it came and the sun shines forth
brilliantly. Then we go down the sides
of the ancient and blood-stained Pyramid
of Cholula and return to Pueblo de los
Angelos in—a street car.

CHAPTER XV.

CITY OF MEXICO.

"TRAINS down here are so very po-
lite," that this one takes at least
half an hour backing and blowing, snorting
and puffing, apologizing, so to speak, for
the enforced intrusion on the depot grounds,
ere it finally comes to a standstill. We
know by seeing every one connected with
it suddenly roll themselves in their serapes
and go to sleep, that we have reached
our destination, or at least that it will be
some hours before any of that gang can
be induced to move further. Bestirring
ourselves and collecting our belongings—
such as have survived the day—we emerge
dust-laden and smoke-begrimed into the
silence of this old city. Profoundly asleep,

even as though an enchanter had waved
his wand over all, casting man and beast
into slumber only to awaken at the com·
ing of the king. Can this be on the
same continent with New York and
Chicago? or are we indeed in the heart
of old Spain? Long, wide streets stretch
away in every direction before us, on each
side of which rise the square-topped houses
with their heavily barred windows, while
through the doorways we catch a glimpse
now and then of palm and flower em-
bowered Patios. To our right against the
crumbling arches of an old stone aque-
duct rise the grotesque and moss-grown
figures of a great fountain, over whose
stone basins the water has fallen for two
hundred years. That seems a bit of ancient Rome. Before us the dark woods
of the Alameda spread away until they
meet the groves of Chapultepec, where

stands the tree under which Montezuma wept for his lost kingdom; while before and above us faintly gleam the cones of Popocatepetl and Ixtaccihuatl in the shimmering moonlight. Nothing human in sight; nothing to denote that the place is peopled otherwise than with ghosts, unless it be those bundles under the shadow of that door-way, or that form, half animal, with the slouched sombrero and closely wrapped serape that skulks across the deserted square from one bit of shadow to another. Silently we regard it all for a few moments, scarcely daring to venture further into this city of the long ago, until we are reminded by a citizen of the old town, whom we have chanced to meet on the way up, that it would be well to seek an hotel and the protection afforded thereby, as "these people are not friendly." With great difficulty two crazy old cabs are secured; on one of which we load our luggage, while we crawl with great misgivings into the other. Creaking and banging along over the uneven pavements they make noise enough to awaken the dead, but do not in any way disturb the profound repose of the denizens of these houses. Indeed, I fancy when Gabriel blows his trumpet he will here at least be answered by a shrug and the murmuring word "mañana," while the people compose themselves for another nap. Perhaps this eternal sleeping is part of their religion which they must maintain until Montezuma yonder on the mountain comes down unto them, and so long as he sleeps they will sleep, the better to be able to meet him in proper form. At least, one would fancy so here, for not even a barking dog answers the clatter of the worn-out cabs.

CHAPTER XVI.

A SHOWER of blows on the heavily-barred doorway of the Hotel Iturbide finally secures us an entrance, but nothing more. Then the drowsy porter, appearing to regard people who are out at such an uncanny hour as a pack of harmless idiots about whom he need not bother himself, vanishes. We mount, unattended, a vast marble staircase, pass down long silent corridors, gaze through doorways opening into echoing chambers deserted save by a stray moonbeam here and there, or by the many frescoes of forgotten faces on walls and ceilings—faces invisible to us at first, as the darkness in there is palpable. But, throwing aside a casement, floods of moonlight pour

over all, giving seeming life to these people of the past, and much comfort to we
of the present. Now that we are in here,
we mean to remain, so we help ourselves
to rooms and do it well, taking an entire
suite on the grand floor overlooking the
street. Vast rooms, all of them, with a
small bed in one corner and a large square
mat in the center, around which five or
six rocking chairs (the only other furniture
in the room) are in quiet motion as though
our entrance had caused a sudden flight
of their occupants. (You have seen the
same actions on the part of chairs in
many a front hall where you have
appeared suddenly.) The one candle allowed for each room simply makes the
darkness visible, therefore we combine
forces and concentrate all from the different rooms on one table. Then we sit
down and look at each other. Not being

accustomed to these rockers one or two
of us roll over backward. Said action at
least makes us feel more at home, and
the silence is broken by our shouts of
laughter.

" It's somewhere near two A. M. Let
us form a solid phalanx and lock up a half
a mile of this and go to bed."

No sooner said than acted upon, and
the procession moves, each person carrying
a candle. As they pass down the long
vista, it resembles a procession of the
" Holy Church." Each room is examined
separately, and then securely locked and
barricaded. All goes well with the invad-
ing force whose bravery is something un-
excelled. The fate of any enemy would
have been appalling just then. I doubt
if the palace has been occupied since
Iturbide moved out. The silence, which is
certainly overwhelming, is broken only by

EMPEROR ITURBIDE'S HOUSE.

the snarl of some prowling cats. And we thank God there is something alive in this place, though why any first class cats that can move north remain here, is more than we can understand.

So we settle ourselves for what is left of the night, but even as I sink into slumber I hear a distant voice murmur: " Oh, brother, I don't believe papa would ever find us if we were to die here."

CHAPTER XVII.

I F it was quiet last night it is noisy enough this morning. Before daylight the rattle of moving wheels and cries of the market vendors render sleep almost impossible, especially as we have insisted upon sleeping with open windows. A Mexican closes both windows of glass and shutters of iron, the night air being dreaded as much as robbery or murder. The street of the "San Francisco" is a moving mass of people, many carrying huge water jugs or trays of strange looking fruits on their heads. Here comes a dray drawn by four mules abreast. There go a party evidently English, out for an early canter. They are gravely saluted by a splendid figure clothed in the national riding cos-

tume, all of fine leather, heavily embroidered in beads and silk, the broad sombrero
glistening with silver lace and a jewel or
two, while saddle and bridle are richly
ornamented—the horse, a fine black animal, seeming thoroughly aware of his
splendid appearance.   Over the way stands
a sleeping donkey who knows too well
that his only chance for rest is to take it
standing.   Across his back his master has
thrown two pig-skins that appear to quiver
and palpitate with life.   Around about are
grouped a lot of wretched people waiting
their turn to be served.   The old man
seizes the neck of a skin, and untieing a
cord wrapped around it, allows the bluish-
white and sour-smelling pulque to run into
the gourds extended to receive it.   In all
my stay in the country I have never been
able to bring myself to taste this liquid.
The sour-smell pervading people and shops

has many a time driven me from places I desired to see. But the natives drink it down with great gusto. How thoroughly foreign every thing is, and how ancient, yet this is on the same continent with our own bustling modern nation.

I am recalled from the window by a clatter on our doors, and open to find our luggage bearers. Thank goodness! To have donned again those dust ladened, sea-soaked clothes would have been any-thing save pleasant. By numerous signs we make it understood that baths are wanted, and are conducted down many stairways into the bowels of the earth, where we find a row of rooms, each with a tub so enormously deep that we seize convulsively the edge, thinking that there can be no bottom at all. The water was cool and clear when we entered, but not

so when we came out. If cleanliness is
one of the items upon which man is
judged, I am most happy in that said
judgment was deferred in our cases until
after these baths, or none of us would
have ranked near unto "godliness." We
have not looked respectable for so long
that our rejuvenation is a cause of deep
satisfaction. Out in the sunny court-yard,
in little huts of bark, covered with trail-
ing vines, breakfast is served. Baskets of
fruit, the green cherry moya, the yellow
granaditta, the luscious pine and golden
orange, followed by an omelet à fillet
and good coffee, though generally I do
not like either the Mexican coffee or
chocolate. After all we conclude that
Mexico is a land of the living, else
whence come these good things to eat
and who cooks them? What a small
world it is after all—as just here I raise

my eyes and standing in the doorway
see two ladies, friends whom I have not
seen since I left them at the foot of
Mount Tabor in the Holy Land years
ago. The meeting is most pleasant, and
we cease to feel so entirely as "strangers
in a strange land." After all, it is the
people, not the place, that make the
home, and to one who wanders the wide
world over, making friends in all quarters,
the world at large soon becomes "home."

CHAPTER XVIII.

THIS visit to Mexico occurs at a time when people from the "States" are few and far between. It is just after an expedition from our land which did not leave the best impression upon the minds of the Mexicans. Our first walk is much like a procession, especially does one of the ladies attract attention. Her deep mourning seemingly upsets the populace. Later we learn that the Mexican women never leave the house during the period of mourning, and rarely, if ever, walk. We are in search of better quarters. The hotel is cold and barren and would not be pleasant for a prolonged stay, and we must remain in the city until the next ship from Vera Cruz, three weeks hence. In our quest we are most fortunate, and from our entrance into the house of Mrs. Gadsden, No. 7 Seminario, dates one of the most delightful periods of our lives. It is on the great square next to the Palace, across from the parish church and the great cathedral, and occupies the entire "grand" or upper floor. Beneath it live a senator with his family, a big yellow cat and a large green parrot. Below them on the ground floor and around the Patio the concierge and sundry families of professional beggars hold sway, the latter always giving the inhabitants of "their upper floors" the preference in the matter of donating alms, and with an air which assures us that they consider that we are all of one family,—" God forbid !"

From the balcony of our rooms we overlook the entire city, and away on all sides to the grand wall of encircling mountains, over which, like two hoary-headed sentinels

THE CATHEDRAL BY MOON-LIGHT.

on guard, tower Popocatapetl and Ixtaccihuatl. Many an evening we assemble on
the house-top to watch the sun go down,
and witness the sudden falling of the night
on this wondrous panorama. On all sides
spread the flat-roofed gaily-colored Spanish
city, through whose midst broad avenues
stretch away in all directions, and above
which the campaniles of the many churches
mount high in air. Just before us those of
the great cathedral are most conspicu-
ous. That dark circle near the base of the
one on the left is the famous calendar stone
of the Aztecs. In the court of the museum
beneath one can faintly see the outlines
of the sacrificial stone, which, in the days
of Montezuma, crowned the Teocalli, that
stood where is now the public square. It
is only three hundred years since the cries
of agony from human victims rang out over
this fair valley, since the blood of their sac-

rifices flowed in torrents down the steps of
stone. The cross has banished all that, but
just behind us rise the towers of the church
of Santo Domingo, in whose walls were
found the withered remains (now in the
museum) of two poor human beings,—the
one a little girl—who had been immured,
and who had starved and smothered to
death in slow agony. Surely the Aztecs
could teach the priests of the cross nothing
in the matter of cruelty. But, thank God,
that was long ago. Now you may walk the
streets of this fair city and be in danger
from no religion; but it would not be safe
to go out after dark. These people are
assassins and thieves of the worst order.
They will not attack a party, but do not go
alone. The shadows are already thick in
the arcades below us, but the lakes which
surround the capital gleam brightly in the
reddening light as the sun sinks. Off

beyond the green Alameda stretches the avenue to Chapultepec, whose towers crown the summit of a distant hill; beyond which one can just discern the spot where the terrible battle of " Molino del Rey" occurred in 1847. Off to the right the cemetery and shrine of Guadalupe crowns the summit of one of the foot hills. It was there that the Virgin showed herself to Indian John. The sun is going down like a great yellow ball. A sudden pause seems to have fallen over the life of the city. Vast flocks of vultures are slowly settling on the domes of the churches— all things appear as though waiting for some change. It comes, suddenly and swiftly—the curtain of the night—wrapping all things in darkness, while it casts over man and beast a mantle of profound slumber, to which many of them having no homes yield instantly, and sink

on the pavements, where they will remain until morning. Only the tips of the
higher mountains flame out like great light-
houses, but even they soon desert their
posts, and a mantle of darkness most profound wraps the Kingdom of Montezuma in
its folds.

CHAPTER XIX.

THE flat below us, occupied by the senator, is *en fête* to-night, which, for some reason, strangely excites our dog, "Palomo." He has been crazy to get down there, and has been impatiently waiting for some one to open our stair doorway, which I do on the sly. The result is disastrous. With a bark and a rush he descends like greased lightning. I see him enter their kitchen door and hear a most tremendous powwow, followed by a clattering and much noise. Has he bitten the cook, I wonder? The commotion is not stationary, nor confined to the kitchen, but progresses from room to room. At last I see a yellow streak closely pursued by a black and white streak flying round and round the banquet

hall, under the table, over the feet of the
excited guests, until with a final bark of
triumph, Palomo drives the cat up one of
the pillars of the patio and rushes himself
up our staircase to safety and me, whom he
finds convulsed with laughter in a dark
corner.   I never saw any thing more expressive or human than the actions of that
dog on his return,   Such delighted eyes,
such tail-waggings.   Forever after it was
only necessary to call once, and he would
rush for the stairs and never return until he
had found that cat, no matter what he broke
in the finding.   Many a time I have seen
the "senatorial dignitary" sitting cross-
legged on the table for safety's sake.   Poor
Palomo, he has long since gone to the "Isle
of Dogs," which must surely be the canine
heaven, where I hope he may renew his
youth now and then by meeting a yellow
cat.

CHAPTER XX.

THE next morning en route to our legation we pass through the great square before the cathedral, and are at once reminded of poor Carlotta, as she it was who caused the planting of all these trees, making the spot one of beauty. But beautiful though it is *now*, it was in the ancient days one of horror, for here stood the great Teocalli. At the portals of the cathedral we pause a moment to inspect the bird market. No end of chattering, singing parrots. But to my ear the most beautiful notes in the world are produced by the little gray clarine, a bird somewhat larger than our pestiferous sparrow and of a slate color.

But, oh the music of its voice! I remember one line of an old song that well describes it:

"'T is the voice of the mermaid as she sings 'neath the
    sea."

If mortals could descend to old ocean's caverns they would expect to hear just such gurgling music.

Entering this great church, towering so grandly above me, I am again convinced that Mexico holds the only "cathedrals" on our continent. We have many beautiful "churches" at home, but they are not worthy to be called cathedrals. But in the sanctuaries of Pueblo and this city one finds cathedrals that equal most in the old world and are surpassed by but few. Vast in size, most stately in appearance, and decorated in the richest marbles—you can not but wonder how

such structures could have been erected
on our new continent at such a period.
The interior of this one is dotted with
the usual motley congregation, gathered
here and there before some altar or shrine.
Before me there kneels an old man deeply
engaged in his devotions, which are inter-
rupted by the woman next to him trying
to steal his handkerchief. I suppose she
thinks that as he is fool enough to allow
it to stick out he deserves to have it
stolen. However, some one, his wife at
home probably, has provided for just some
such an emergency by pinning it in. The
remarks exchanged between the two in no
way upset the service and draw little or
no attention from the other worshipers,
while the droning voice of the priest keeps
evenly onward; though I doubt not he
has spotted the would-be thief and will
make her do penance, probably pay for

a mass or two. The great altar glitters with marble, gold and silver, and high overhead on the blue vault of the dome hosts of painted priests, angels and children tumble around in the most surprising confusion. I suppose the whole is typical of the painter's idea of Heaven, but I hope he is wrong. Those positions are absurd, no matter what the pleasure may be.

As we gaze aloft the bells in the tower commence to wheeze and groan and jangle. All the Mexican bells are cracked and their melody, if it ever existed, is all gone long ago. Perhaps the wrangle and jangle which they have been forced to keep up during the numerous revolutions is the cause thereof; as the alarm is always given on them, and the party that secures the tower where they hang generally car-

CALENDAR STONE.
(Since removed to the Museum.)

ries the day. Many a revolt has been
prevented by a word to the custodian,
who securely bars the entrance. Nothing
rouses these Mexicans save the sound of
these particular bells. We do not wonder; just now the discord would arouse
the devil, and yet they are more in ac-
cord with the general condition of things
here. Sweet bells would sound out of
place and soon be jangled out of tune.

Low on the outer walls of one of the
towers hangs the huge stone calendar of
the Aztecs, or rather it is imbedded in the
wall. Its cabalistic signs and figures are
as sharp in outline as when first it left
the hands of its makers. When and where
was that I wonder? Perhaps it is as old
as the ruins of Egypt. No one knows
surely. When you cross the court-yard
of the museum near by and stand by the

great sacrificial stone, surrounded by the gods of the past, it is not hard to imagine the scenes of the sacrifices. On top of a great square pyramid of steps stood this altar. On top of it was placed a small block over which the victim was stretched, throwing the region of the heart well up. With one stroke of a sharp pointed stone the priest cut open the body, tore out the living heart and held it aloft to the people, while over the steps gushed the crimson life blood of him who a moment before had mounted the Teocalli—a perfect specimen of manhood, for none other was acceptable to their gods. For weeks he had lived on the fat of the land and been housed in the Holy of Holies, while the most beautiful maidens of the city were brought unto him. At last, garlanded with flowers, decked in a rich dress of feathers, he slowly mounted the

Teocalli to the sound of many gongs and much barbaric music. He knew what was coming; he knew that each step brought him nearer to that awful stone; that ere long the sunshine would be shut forever from his sight; that his splendid body through which the life blood was bounding so freely would be feasted on by the priests around him. Mounting higher and higher he cast aside as he moved his rich robes, broke his musical instruments, and tore his garlands to pieces. All the while grim and ghastly gods stared upon him in seemingly malignant mirth, and the discordant voice of the high priest expounded the example of his life to the people.

"Though begun in glory, it is ending in gloom."

But that end came quickly and with no torture. A sudden, swift movement threw him backward across the stone, the flint glittered for an instant in the hands of the high priest, and then the crimson life blood gushed in torrents down the steps of the Teocalli, over the broken musical instruments and soaked the garments of by-gone splendor, while his still quivering heart was held aloft before the worshiping multitudes as they bathed hands and faces in his blood. Yet all this, and all that follows does not fill one with half such shuddering horror as one glimpse at that poor little distorted figure, so lately found in the walls of the Santo Domingo.

CHAPTER XXI.

THOUGH some seven thousand feet above the sea, Mexico is far from healthy. Low fevers prevail in summer, and the waters are poisonous. At least one attributes the bowel troubles that are apt to attack strangers to that source. To sit in a draft is also dangerous, nor is it safe to be out after dark. The weather was simply superb, and we had excellent health while there, but when I returned some years later, all the people whom I had known on my former visit had either gone north or were in the graveyard—the latter a large majority. You must dress warmly always, and it is not safe to change from heavy to light clothing or *vice versa.* In fact the climate seemed to me like that of

Rome. The altitude always affects one at first, and came near driving us home.

The fevers of the place are easily accounted for. The city lies lower than the lakes which surround it, and during the rainy season the water rises several feet in the streets and courts, and on this floats the scum of the sewage. So don't come here during the rains (the summer). It is feared that, when the great system of drainage now in hand is completed, much of the town will dry up and collapse. But no improvements were even contemplated when I first visited the place. It was as it had been for centuries, and I know did not relish the awakening which came shortly after. Those at home who shout so constantly for annexation should come down and see these people, when they might in some degree appreciate the hopelessness

of a union of any sort. We have not a
thought or feeling in common. Their ways
are not and never will be as ours. Possessing as they do strong traits of their savage
ancestry, we never can be in touch with
them. We must wipe them out utterly and
begin with a new race. They are not in
the least like the few Spaniards who enter
our ports at the North, but resemble more
the hordes of Egypt and Syria, and I do
not believe it would be any more possible
to dwell together in unity with them, than
with the Indians of the North. They hate
us quite as heartily, and this hatred is fos-
tered and kept alive by an ignorant priesthood, who possess absolute power over the
masses, and knowing that with the advent
of northern ideas would come an end to
all that, they oppose us bitterly, even to the
advising of these poor wretches to fire into
the trains from the North. This happened

as I came from El Paso, in 1887, and the conductor informed me that it was of constant occurrence, and that he had several times stopped the trains and caught the miscreants. · Of course the government is against such a state of affairs and does what it can to stop it, but these ignorant minds are only governed by their priests. However, annexation is not an immediate danger, so let us leave it.

FUNERAL VAULT OF THE IMPERIAL FAMILY.
(Church of the Capuchins, Vienna.)

CHAPTER XXII.

INTO the gloomy vaults of the Capuchins in Vienna we entered one summer day, leaving all brightness behind us. Descending the long flights of stone stairs, guided by a monk, who murmured softly the names of the illustrious dead, we paused for a moment before the magnificent sarcophagus of Maria Theresa; then by that of the little King of Rome, and, finally, in a dark corner, where a long ray of sunlight fell full upon it by a lonely sarcophagus, on which lay a wreath of immortelles. Stooping to see who had remembered the royal dead, we read on a card the name " Carlotta," and on the bronze beneath it " Maximilian." Instantly my

thoughts flew westward over ocean and
mountains to the court-yard of the old
palace of Mexico, where stood the gorgeous gilded coach, given to the ill-fated
Empress by the Emperor of Austria, and
in which, drawn by four white mules, she
used to make her progress to Chapultepec.   Its cushions are not soiled, nor
the gilding tarnished, while she for whom
it was built beats her hands against the
bars of a mad-house in Brussels, as she
murmurs forever the name of her dead
one.   Above it waved the tree, "La
Manieta," while it cast in showers over
the coach its blossoms, shaped like a
human hand of a blood-red color, making
you shudder and draw back as though
the hand of Juarez was still casting the
gauntlet of hatred and defiance at those
poor victims of Napoleon III.

They say in Mexico that Carlotta taunted
Maximilian with the loss of his kingdom
and drove him back to his certain death
—for Juarez had warned him that such
would be his fate if he returned. She
entered her ship at Vera Cruz, but before
he sank a lifeless corpse on the sands
of Queretaro she was a raving maniac,
made so, as it is believed, by poison ad-
ministered by one of her attendants—a
jealous woman. The people in Mexico
loved them both, for they worked constantly, doing nothing save good. But
that would weigh little with Juarez and
the class he represented, as you have
only to look at his portrait—Indian in
every line—to fully understand. It would
have made no difference if Maximilian
and Carlotta had both been natives, that
face would never have spared any thing
that stood in its way. It is an immense

satisfaction to Americans to know that, though we would not permit a monarchy to exist on our continent, or rather the establishment of one by a foreign power, we did our best to save this unfortunate emperor, and but for the fact that the "attractions" of New Orleans overpowered our envoy, who, therefore, never reached Mexico, Juarez would have listened to Seward's remonstrance against that useless murder.

CHAPTER XXIII.

THE sun has just thrown its first searching rays over the rim of the mountains as we start on horseback to visit Chapultepec. The city is not yet awake and bundles of people lie here and there and every-where. In the cathedral square the venders of birds have simply thrown old rebosas (shawls) over the cages and, doubling up on the ground underneath, have gone to sleep. As we pass one parrot's cage Polly is vainly endeavoring to awaken her owner, as she tries to catch sight of him over the rim of her cage, pausing anon to scratch her head and croak at us. We can scarcely distinguish between the gurgling of the fountains and the sweet notes of the clarines. The orange trees are in bloom and the air is full of the odor of over ripened fruit from the market near by. As we pass down the street of the San Francisco we note the strange outlines of the houses. Here is the massive-barred front of the palace, sacred to the memory of the Emperor Iturbide—hallowed also by the memory of our first night's stay in the capital. There, is a fantastic house all of blue porcelain tiles, and yonder is a patio gleaming in many colors of marble; while the next is of pure white, over which flaming Hibiscus and the dainty Passion vine tumble in wild profusion. Now the street widens out, even as the day is widening. Long lines of stately mansions to our left, while to the right stretch away the woods of the Alameda, and before us miles in

extent and magnificent in width is the
grand avenue to Chapultepec, the "Paseo."
With its double rows of trees, its
fountains, and its royal monuments, it
forms an avenue unique and almost un-
rivaled in the world. In fact I know
of none with which to compare it save
that leading up to the arch of the Star,
and this after it leaves the city far sur-
passes the great avenue of Paris—in that
it has a superb view of most stupendous
mountains (18,000 feet in height). It is,
of course, the grand drive of the city. I
have exhibited myself on it several times,
but never with such perfect success as upon
one Easter Sunday. Having ordered my
horse several days before, and commanded
that he be strictly English in his get-
up, banged tail, saddle, etc., etc., I retired
to array myself and came out looking
magnificently—as to clothes ; one of Pooles'

latest productions in fact. Trowsers of
the deepest blue with a broad, black band,
patent leather riding shoes with shining
spurs, a high hat, and an enormous bou-
tonnière of violets. I meant to annihilate
that town. Starting the ladies away in
a landau (thank God, I did) I awaited
my steed. Instead of a thoroughly cor-
rect "Park Hack," I found before me
one of those brown and white splotched
circus animals, so old that his head hung
limp before him and his tail was hairless;
and such a saddle! Words were useless.
It would do no good to swear, as neither
man nor beast understood a word of any
thing save their own vile patois. Even
the cats do not know that they are so
called in a civilized land. However, I
ordered another horse and retreated to
tone down my costume, Started at last,
all went well, comparatively speaking, until

THE BUCARELI PROMENADE OR GRAND AVENUE TO CHAPULTEPEC.

I reached the circle where the band was
discoursing sweet music, then my beast
quietly backed around and alongside of
the rest of the hack horses, all in a
circle around the Pagoda, and though I
spurred, pounded and whipped, and I
confess, swore, he would not move a
muscle until that piece of music was
over. Being accustomed to the huge
Mexican spurs, my little English ones
produced no effect. However, I perse-
vered until I forced the brute in time
to move on, only to go through the
same performance as I returned. There
was not much pleasure in that ride, and
to this day I am treated to side remarks
concerning it. However, that occurred
many years after our first ride to Chapultepec, on which occasion we met with
several parties of English and Americans,
and also with Mexican gentlemen—the

women do not ride—but I notice that all
are in parties, none alone or in couples;
and am informed that it would not be
safe to come here at this hour save in
parties. One has only to glance at those
skulking forms behind that hedge to fully
believe it.

As we enter the groves of Chapultepec (Grasshopper Hill) we pause in
admiration. Huge red cedars, second
only to those of California, stand thickly
around us, while from their lofty branches
the Spanish moss hangs like a silver
veil. In this dry air it attains great
lengths and is white and silvery, as you
never see it in Florida. Over all and
grander than all rises the great tree of
Montezuma. The sun is well up in the
heavens now and throws his glorious light
down the aisles of this grand natural

cathedral, at the further end of which
rise the walls of the palace which stands
on the site of that of the unfortunate
monarch. It is on a small hill, I should
say two hundred feet high, and in the
present building possessing nothing of interest or beauty; but from its ramparts
we see one of the great panoramas of
the world. To my mind there are five
great panoramas which rank on a par:
Cairo and the Nile, Constantinople from
Galàta, Moscow from Sparrow Hill, the
Bay of Naples, and this view from Chapultepec. To this one might add Benares
from the Ganges. This valley is a complete circle, encompassed by these gigantic
mountains, with Chapultepec as a central
point. Before us spreads the white city
with its many campaniles and brilliant
roofs, the nearer lakes gleam in the sunshine, while those afar off by the mount-

ains are dark as night. The lower ranges
of the Cordilleras are deep in shadow,
with here and there slashes of brilliant
blue and purple, while high over all rise
the two great mountains Popocatepetl and
Ixtaccihuatl, glistening brilliantly as they
reflect the rays of the ever-increasing
sunlight. Just behind us is the site of
the battle of Molino del Rey, and over
there to the left the tree of the Noche
Triste. Long aqueducts in stone, centuries old, stretch their arches over the
plains ; while in the middle distance beyond
city and suburbs spread the dusty plains
with their long lines of cacti plants, which
here throw aside all romantic nonsense
concerning the "blossoms of a century,"
etc., etc., and come forth in flower in
from ten to fourteen years time. Then,
having accomplished their mission wither
away root and branch. In the immediate

foreground the avenue of the Paseo leads
eastward until it reaches the Alameda;
and just where they join and where the
trees are so green and thick now, arose
of old the flames of the *auto da fes*.

CHAPTER XXIV.

ALL roads in Mexico seem to lead to Chapultepec, and one comes here again and again to lean over its ramparts and feast the soul with the splendid scene. Its palace has now been fitted up as a residence for the president, gorgeous of course so far as the upholsterer can make it. We see there a very magnificent service of silver, made for the late emperor, but very little else of interest. Still, this is after all the most historic spot in the land, and here the memories of the past gather thickest around us. It was as dear to the Aztecs as was Granada to the Moors. In that grove below us were buried their monarchs. Where we stand they dwelt for centuries. The child-like Montezuma passed the happiest years of his life here, and here he first received tidings of the coming of those strangers who were to end all things for him. Dark dreams had disturbed his rest. Earthquakes and eruptions marred the fair valley of his royal city. His greatest temple was destroyed by fire. Then, as he gazed out over the same scene smiling so serenely before us to-day, he beheld his people driven almost mad with superstitious terror. In vain were the human sacrifices so freely offered. In vain the religious feasts and dances. The hour had come and the little fleet of ships stealing so quietly up the coast was bringing the men who were to subdue the millions of the land. They say that at night even now, all up and down that avenue leading to the tree of the Noche Triste yonder, phantom hosts battle unceasingly, and in the moon-light Cortez can still be seen weeping over all he has lost—mourning over the dead and dying around him. While below us, beneath the shadow of that great cedar with its veil of silvery moss, the ghostly figure of the Atzec monarch lies prone in agony. His garments of many colored feathers torn and disordered. His crown of plumes crushed into nothingness, while he, like Boabdil-el-Chico, weeps even as a woman over that which he could not defend like a man. Truly these avenues of Chapultepec are ghost haunted. Misty nights bring out the restless spirit of Iturbide, while through the star-lit isles the shadowy figure of Maximilian passes with bowed head, and from his lips again are heard those last words as he sank at Queretaro, "Oh man, man!" When the winds are out the sad voice of Carlotta

is wafted from terrace to terrace in long
peals of demoniacal laughter. Lightning
flashes over the half savage faces of Santa
Anna and his merciless crew, while the
rattle of thunder brings back the spirits
of our own boys in blue over there on
the field of Molino del Rey where they
fell so bravely. All that, they say, can be
seen and heard at night when the moonlight and stormlights chase each other
round the "Hill of the Grasshopper." But
now as the full light of the noon-day sun
strikes down upon Chapultepec, she is the
center of a realm of peace and beauty,
while around the old tree of the Atzec
monarch a band of dark-eyed, scarlet-robed
Mexican children have joined hands and
are dancing in and out of its waving
mosses to the sound of the mandolin.
The balmy air is laden with the odor of

the magnolia, so heavy, so sweet, that one's senses are wafted into slumber, rendered deeper and more profound by the singing of many birds and the gurgling sound of falling waters.

GREAT TREE OF MONTEZUMA AND THE CASTLE OF CHAPULTEPEC.

CHAPTER XXV.

I SHOULD warn all travelers who come to Mexico to bring letters of credit and not drafts, as it is almost impossible to have the latter cashed. No amount of identification seems to satisfy these bankers, who appear to imagine that the end and aim of the people from the States is to swindle them.

It was our fortune, good or bad as you please, to arrive just as an excursion from the north was departing, and we were furnished with much amusement at the many promises left behind, and by the general state of indignation caused by many actions new and strange to the inhabitants of this ancient city. They could not imagine that even in the rush and roar of the vast City of Chicago, not only the promises made to them, but even the visit to their city would soon be forgotten utterly or remembered only as some thing afar off and dream like. On the occasion of that visit the contents of that great curiosity shop—the national pawn shop— were opened and dusted. It is amongst the most curious of the many places in the town. There every thing from a sauce-pan to a necklace of diamonds can be found. It is claimed that most of the jewels of the country are here in pawn, and when, on the occasion of the ball given at that time, the ladies of the city wished to appear in all their glory, they drove to the pawn shop on their way to the ball, and, leaving horses and carriages as pledges, were allowed the use of their jewels for that night only. Not having time to clean them, the effect on their fair arms and shoulders was in a short time startling. I do not consider the women of Mexico beautiful, and the manner in which they pile on the powder until their faces are deathly, is most unpleasant to one from the north, while the ghastly effect is increased by the stare of great black glassy eyes. However, I fancy their men must admire it or it would scarcely be done. I notice also that here the language of old Castile which in the mother country sounded so silvery and beautiful, is harsh and clattering, and when one is at all unwell, utterly unbearable. As you walk about you stumble now and then on a figure strangely like the celebrated "Mr. Guppy." Thin to gauntness, with sunken eyes and disheveled hair, he leans with folded arms against some house corner or door-post, while his eyes are fastened constantly upon some neighboring window behind which you faintly discern the shadowy form of a woman. This is the Spanish mode of courtship, and is called "bearing." It goes on for some weeks, after which, if he is accepted by the parents, he is admitted to the house and an interview with them, not with the adored one. He never sees her alone until he marries her. I was so deeply interested in one case yesterday that I inadvertently stepped upon a pulque skin, bursting it open and flooding the pavement with the disgusting liquid. Most demonstrative was the sorrow of the owner until I bought his silence, while my own disgust was equally intense as the odor clung to my shoes for days. That was the only time I ever attacked the national drink.

CHAPTER XXVI.

WE went this morning to visit the tomb of Juarez. Under a white marble canopy lies a full length figure of this slayer of Maximilian, and as you gaze upon the face, Indian in every line, you fully understand that having warned the Emperor that return meant death, this was a man to keep his word. The high cheek bones, long straight black hair, and broad nose, all go toward the make up of a face to be found any day amongst our northern tribes. His daughters, whom we met at the legation, are strangely like him. If I remember rightly, they were educated in our country. One can not blame the Mexicans for resisting foreign

force and rule, yet it is claimed here that
the people were devoted to Maximilian
and Carlotta—only those of Juarez' rank
causing all the trouble. We have met
several times the tall sorrowful figure of
the Empress Iturbide, another victim of
the third Napoleon. I could not but remember her as I watched in '91 an old
and bowed figure, clothed in rusty mourning, seated on an iron stool in the garden
of the Tuilleries, while the eyes, all that
remained of the once glorious beauty of
Eugénie, gazed mournfully on the site of
her former triumphs. She is not of suffi-
cient consequence now for the French
government to object to her presence.

Out beyond the tomb of Juarez we
came upon one of the old stone aqueducts
that still bring the blessings of water to
the people. There are several of these

THE SPOUTING FOUNTAIN.

structures all in perfect condition. They are not so lofty as those of Rome, but all terminate in beautiful moss-grown stone fountains, around whose basins you find a constant crowd of people, though I do not think that they can have any capacity for water, after all the pulque they drink—and they certainly never bathe.

CHAPTER XXVII.

ASIDE from a drive on the Alameda
or to Chapultepec, you rarely use
a carriage here. Tram cars of all classes
run through most of the streets and far
into the suburbs, to Guadalupe, to Tacubaya, and many other points; in fact, such
is the condition of the streets, that you
must use them if you would go at all.

Starting one morning about nine o'clock,
we found in the great square our minister
and his wife, Monsieur and Madam M——
(now secretary of state), and some others
(on invitation), and boarding a car for Tacubaya, spent a most delightful day under
the trees of the Baron and Escandone

estates. They were truly beautiful places.
The house of the former is of two stories,
and stretches at great length along a
marble terrace, on whose steps and balus-
trades stand urns filled with flowers, while
through the vistas of the park the falling
waters of many fountains make the air
musical. The house itself is filled with
all that wealth, possessed for generations,
combined with good taste, can purchase.
Here, a boudoir with dainty fittings of
malachite; there, a library whose shelves
are crammed to the top. On the fly-leaf
of the first book I picked up was written,
"With the compliments of the author,
Henry W. Longfellow." A room in which
one might study and dream a life away,
the world forgetting, with no regret that
they were "by the world forgot."

Down a long vista of hallway, through

a lofty portal, the rays of light struck upon gilded frames and the rich warm tints of the many paintings—old masters and new—and as is usual in most large galleries, good, bad, and indifferent, though as a whole these were good, and were a collection always impossible in any land where the law of primogeniture has never existed. (I am not certain that it exists there now, though it did not long since.) We spent several hours wandering over the interesting place, and having little or nothing to do with each other, each following the bent of his or her own tastes, information and inclinations. It was all open, the family being in Europe, but as they were personal friends of our minister, we had the freedom of the house.

I finally wandered into a deep bay of the library, evidently a favorite nook of

some of the dead and gone owners. A
small table and a large easy chair stood
in the corner. Through the stained-
glass windows the long rays of sunlight
threw the shadows of waving leaves across
the thorn-crowned face that Guido Reni
painted. Silence and the soothing music
of a fountain soon sent me nodding over
my book. Don't be shocked when I tell
you it was Ouida's " Puck." I was suddenly aroused by deep breathing and sniff-
ing, and found myself under watch and
guard of an immense bloodhound. I had
the good sense not to move, and for some
moments man and beast stared straight
into each other's eyes. It is claimed the
old notion that the human eye can cow
and subdue that of a beast is all nonsense,
but I fully believe it, though I do not think
it would save one's life. Still in this case
it was but a moment ere the superb ani-

mal growlingly lowered his eyes and head, and at last settled on the floor near by, ever and anon casting savage glances in my direction, but shifting them away at once on meeting mine. I did not, it is useless to say, attempt to escape. Fortunately the strong sunlight which poured into one of the windows, threw us both into bold relief, and caused one of the servants to come to my succor.

Breakfast had been spread on the terrace. We had evidently drawn from the resources of the house, as the silver and glass, all of the most exquisite quality and workmanship, bore the family arms, and by their beauty added much to the enjoyment of the feast.

Later, as we were gathered in the bowl-ing alley, we suddenly found that we had as companions not one, but three immense bloodhounds, and then it was explained that the people of these places keep them as guards against kidnappers. Even with such protection they are not always safe (in 1879), as was demonstrated not long since by the sudden disappearance of one of the rich men of the city. He was almost given up as dead when a little child asked the searchers if they were "looking for the man under the bed;" there he was found, not under the bed, but under the floor, bound, gagged, and almost dead with starvation. I doubt if the city under Montezuma was half as dangerous a place of residence as during the late years. Now, 1890, it is far different, thanks to the introduction of northern life, steam, etc., with the many other improvements that always follow in their train. Yet I am glad I saw the land before all that happened. Strangers in those days were few and far between, and welcomed with open arms by the upper classes. Now they are numberless, and in consequence, the people have retired unto themselves. You see nothing of them unless especially presented. But all that has nothing to do with those bloodhounds that appeared at last to realize that we were friends, not foes. Two went to sleep, but my old guardian approached and laid his great head with its horrible fangs on my knee, while his expressive eyes seemed to ask my pardon for his late conduct. I granted it by a gentle caress, and he sealed the compact by an energetic wag of his tail. Is there any thing on earth more expressive than a dog's tail? I certainly can never forget the intense watchfulness of that old guard as he stood over me in the library. Its expression was tremen-

dous. It was just as expressive in the
bowling-alley as it whacked a friendly rata-
plan on my thinly clad back. Shortly there-
after he caused the very objectionable fat
woman from Indiana to almost faint away
as he dashed with a roar after the ball that
had just left her hands.

The sun was sinking fast before we
moved to leave that abode of peace. As
I stood on the long marble terrace and
looked my last on its beauty, regret at
parting was strong upon me. Surrounded
by its high walls, it was so secluded from
the world, so shut off from the rush and
roar of the country, that I found there
that quiet, that restful delight, which only
comes now and then in life. I found it
once afterward, in the gardens of the
Taj, in far away India, and again I would
have lingered on forever.

But in the tropics night comes fast, and
the way between Tacubaya and the city is
not safe under her shadows. So we moved
on, leaving this poem in white marble with
the evening sunlight glistening on its leaves
and fountains and lighting up the windows
of its deserted rooms. It was a bit of
Italy dropped by mistake on this western
continent; but, unlike Italy, in that we
could not remain to enjoy it by moonlight.
Indeed, I have no recollections of the beau-
ties of Mexico under the light of the moon,
unless it be a vista of silent street or deserted plaza, or perhaps the outlines of the
old cathedral just opposite my window. This
is because you can not wander off there
alone or even in couples after night falls. It
is neither healthy nor safe, and I maintain
that there is no joy in the moonlight or the
silence of the night if one must be sur-

rounded by a crowd. I also noticed that amongst the people there was little or no love of music, no strolling bands of singers, such as one meets with all over Italy, and I thank God no mechanical pianos. Now and then you see the people dancing the fandango, and in the middle and upper classes hear the music of the Danza; but for the masses life seems to hold no music, save such as is furnished them by the band on the Paseo, and across their watchful, mournful faces you never see the shadow of a smile.

I think the absence of a love for music and their ever-silent watchfulness must come from their Indian blood. Spain certainly was full of music. I remember much of it in Cuba; but these masses do not in the least resemble the people of either of those countries; but rather, as I have said before, the swarms of Egypt and Syria. Like them

in dress, at least among the women, greatly
like them in their silent watchfulness, possessing the same dog-trot movement, which
they will keep up all day long, but which
does not in the least resemble the stately
stalk of the northern Indians.

Apropos of mechanical pianos. One au-
tumn, in Naples, at the Hotel Bristol, we
were so tormented by their horrible clatter
that in deep despair I endeavored to purchase silence. You can imagine the result.
The "fraternity" at once formed a joint
stock concern. I had no sooner bought off
one fiend than another would appear from
around the corner. I did not discover their
game until silence had been purchased three
times. The fourth man looked familiar, and
on closer inspection I found that he was the
first of the gang, and had merely turned his
old hat wrong side out in order to deceive

me, which he evidently felt sure of doing, as his self-composure was immense. Retiring in disgust, I summoned the waiter, and ordered him to bring a half-dozen "bad eggs." He retired, and in a few moments the head waiter appeared, and with vast dignity informed me that "this hotel does not keep that kind." Though convulsed with laughter, I managed to seize a pitcher full of water and to make for the balcony, outside of which the noise and clatter was momentarily growing louder and more triumphant. However, piano and man vanished like the mists of morning as I raised my engine of war aloft. Quiet soon reigned supreme, but I never regained my standing with the head waiter after that order for "bad eggs."

CHAPTER XXVIII.

EVENING brings a reception at the Legation, a cosmopolitan affair most certainly. As we enter we are greeted by our genial host and hostess, who present us to most of the Mexican 400; also to the English, French and American contingent. Those two dark-browed heavy-featured women at the piano are the daughters of the Juarez, next by their side a Spanish matron sits robed in yellow satin and black lace. Yonder are two American ladies, mother and daughter, whom I saw on the sacred Nile; and with that English officer I passed a pleasant week in the Halls of the Alhambra. The orchestra is playing the waltz, "Auf Wiedersehen," its dreamy music has proven too much for that young American girl, who, though in the deepest mourning and almost shrouded in crêpe, is drifting around in the arms of a dark-eyed Spaniard.

The fat woman from Hoosierdom is comparing all and every one to those she knows on the banks of the Wabash, much to the credit of the latter. I hear her discussing a church fair in Evansville as I pass her. She has nothing to do with me as she blames me for that affair of the bloodhound and ball. The wife of the Secretary of State, a beautiful blonde, and by the way an American, is gayly chatting with an English doctor. Ah! there are the strains of the "Danza." How quickly its music draws all into the mazes of the dance until the nations of the earth here commingled, forget for the nonce that they have been and may again be enemies.

CHAPTER XXIX.

WITH ordinary care Mexico is a safe
place to visit. The altitude may
trouble you some, but Jalapa and Orizaba
on the outer rim of this basin are considered
amongst the most healthy places on the
globe, and are but a few hours off. I can
testify to that of Orizaba. It is most charming. The thermometer remains at about
60 degrees the year round, and our roses
bloom in great masses, tumbling over
houses and walls in boundless profusion,
while the air is forever full of that fresh,
sweet odor, so prevalent in our spring
months. If you like tarantulas they have
them there. I was told that on the
Sunday previous to our visit, one had

SACRIFICIAL STONE.

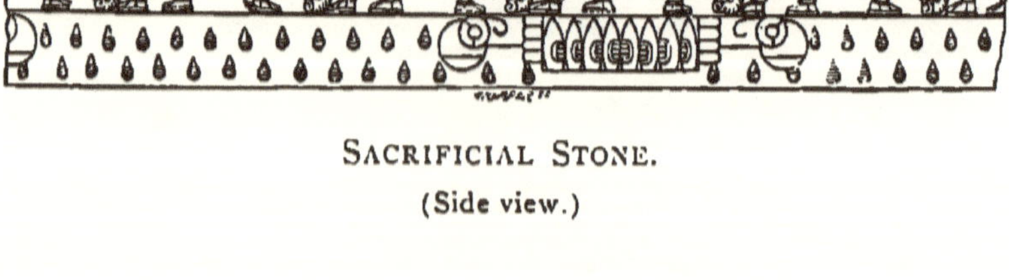

SACRIFICIAL STONE.

(Side view.)

jumped onto the keys of the organ. Orizaba is modern enough to be comfortable. You will find nothing very ancient in the town; in fact, there are very few relics of the Aztec even in the capital. The calendar is in the wall of the cathedral (since removed to the museum), and in one court in the palace are to be found the remainder. Amongst the latter the famous Sacrificial Stone, from the Teocalli of the capital, the same upon which, amongst thousands of natives, many of the men of the conquest were offered up. It is some twenty feet in diameter and four feet thick, with a basin in its center to hold the blood. It is entirely covered with Aztec carvings, and is of a marble hard as flint, and mottled green and black. It is really a work of beauty. Around about stand numerous gods and other images, all in stone. Passing upward into the galleries, the first

thing one sees is an immense painting of
Maximilian, thrown on its side in a corner,
and with several holes through the canvas.
He must have been a very handsome man.
Here he is pictured in full uniform, mounted
on a white charger. The brow is high and
crowned by a mass of yellow hair, while a
long golden beard covers his breast. Eyes
of blue give a pleasant effect to the face.
It is handsome but weak, not unlike that of
"Unser Fritz," and I think that the charac-
ters of the two men were much alike. It
was certainly necessary that this man should
receive the crown of martyrdom to avoid the
utter oblivion of time, but I fancy could he
have been allowed his choice, he would
gladly have exchanged the fleeting glories
of his earthly crown and his crown of martyrdom for a peaceful, happy life in his
beautiful palace of Miramar, with the blue
Adriatic murmuring at its feet. When he

fell, wounded to death at Queretaro, the poor Indians who were present wept aloud, and rushing forward, wiped up every drop of blood. Even in his burial I think he was unfortunate, and if he could have spoken, would have preferred remaining here on the beautiful hills of Mexico, where God's sunlight and storm could pass over him, to being taken to the gloomy vaults of the Capuchins, where that sunlight never comes save in stray beams ; where every sarcophagus around is laden with the bronze images of death ; where no sound is ever heard save the droning voice of monks reciting the merits and titles of the royal dead after the names of nearly every one of whom, from Maria Theresa—broken-hearted over the loss of Silesia—to the late Prince Rudolph, you can write the word "unfortunate."

CHAPTER XXX.

MEXICO possesses really a very fine picture gallery. It occupies several large rooms, and is for the most part, made up of good canvases gathered in the suppression of the monasteries. I remember two that particularly impressed me. One contained two figures, "Dante and Virgil" gazing into the mouth of hell —the reflection therefrom casting a crimson glow over their wondering faces; in the other, "Crazy Joan" wandering over her kingdom with the encoffined body of her husband Phillip Le Bell. The cortege has paused on some wild plain of old Castile, and the figure of the crazy queen stands over the coffin of her husband, while the bleak wind blows her long hair across her vacant, melancholy face; the courtiers stand about regarding her with awe-stricken glances, but she is oblivious to all save her dead. The picture haunts one. I remember standing once in the vaults of the Cathedral of Grenada when it was hard to realize that my hands were resting on the coffins of Ferdinand and the gentle Isabella, while just beyond stood the same coffin that is in this picture, and she who here watches it slept by its side. The scene comes back to me as I gaze now. I remember that in the treasury above were the crown and jewels that Isabella sold to help Columbus, and near by the sword of Boabdil el Chico, the last of the Moors. In my fancy I still hear the murmuring waters of the brooks of Grenada and the silver tones of the bell hung centuries ago in a tower of the

Alhambra—hung there by the Moors to regulate the irrigation of the valley; but no, this sound is cracked and discordant and comes from those of Santa Domingo, the church of the Jesuits. We have just seen in the museum here the two bodies taken from her walls, the one a man, the other a woman, small and delicate, immured by those who worship the memory of Christ, the Compassionate. They had slowly starved to death. The horror of it all makes us shudder as we gaze at the twisted figures and distorted faces, dear both of them to somebody once, and now an eternal reproach to a church guilty of barbarities greater than those of the Aztecs.

CHAPTER XXXI.

MEXICO is full of churches—one in almost every square—and all more or less like the great cathedral, which, strange to say, in this one-time province of old Spain, is much more in the Italian style of architecture than the Spanish. It is grand, but it does not approach those of Seville, Toledo, or Burgos, but is very like that of Maria Maggiore in Rome. I fancy the occupation of the masses has changed but little all these centuries. As we walked through a side street, pausing a moment at a low doorway through which our eyes had been attracted by a sudden gleam of color, we found a lot of men and women engaged on their famous feather work—an art handed down to them by their Aztec ancestors.

One of them showed me a small card on which he had worked a peacock perched on the limb of a tree, all made entirely of feathers. It was much more perfect than painting. Card after card was handed up until we were forced to believe that they must be possessed of a copy of Audubon, as many of the birds were of other climes. Here was also their wonderful figure work in clay. Groups of people and animals— beautiful all of it; but, like so much else from other parts of the globe, it will not endure in our climate. I was much amused to notice some Americans haggling among themselves and with the dealer, over some second-hand work from Paris and which we could not convince them was not Mexican, all the while utterly ignoring the really beautiful native work. I noticed on a later visit that the feather work had lost much of its beauty, caused, I fancy, by the influx of strangers and the consequent greater demand. The natives knowing that they could sell all they made, no matter how poor the work, ceased to take any pains therewith.

CHAPTER XXXII.

ONE morning, passing with Bishop Riley through the sunlit square of the great cathedral, we pause a moment to purchase a couple of the clarines, and are surprised to find that a circus has set up its canvas walls right under the doors of the sanctuary. On closer inspection, it is discovered that " Ben," the educated pig, and his friend, the dancing goose, have deserted the shades of Saratoga for brighter fortunes in this south-ern clime. I chanced, some weeks later, to be on a ship with this celebrated pair, when both were gloriously sea-sick. Giving them the go-by now, however, and disregarding the bombardments of the venders of parrots, paroquets, tortillas (cakes), pilgrim flowers, gorgeous sombreros and serapes, pictures of the Virgin, wreaths of orange blossoms, etc., we pass onward for a look at the new church lately acquired by the bishop from the Catholics. He had had much to say about it, and seemed very proud of his purchase; but alack, on arrival we find that his enemies have stolen the pipes of the organ. From there we visit Mrs. Hooker and her orphanage. What a time the poor woman has of it, to be sure! No sooner settled in one place than through the power of the Roman Catholic Church she is bundled on, bag and baggage. Still, nothing discouraged, she tries again. So it has been for years and will always be, I fancy, until her poor thin hands shall have given up the battle—until her tired ears shall hear the command, "Well done; enter into the joy of thy Lord." She is destined, however, to labor in this vineyard for years to come.

I have not heard of her death, and I met her again in 1888, when she had much to say concerning the mistaken policy of sending clothes and other supplies to this far off city. The cost of transportation being so immense, she is often forced to refuse the cases, their contents being of little or no value, and nearly always unsuitable to this climate. A little money goes a long way in her hands, but any thing else is more of a burden than a blessing. Speaking of the cost of transportation, the story is told of an American woman who came here to live shortly after this railway was opened.* Desiring a cooking stove, she ordered one from the north, the original cost being something like $30, and the bill for transportation nearly $180. We paid $30 for extra luggage between here and El Paso on three

* The Mexican Central.

moderate sized trunks, though we held three first-class tickets.   I have just learned (1893) that Mrs. Hooker has passed away, but not until she had secured that desire of her heart, a building for her "orphan children," a place that the Church of Rome could not turn her out of.   Her children are safe at last, and she rests from her labors.

CHAPTER XXXIII.

THE dead are treated with scant ceremony among the poor, as we discovered this morning. Hearing that a child,
a little girl, daughter of our concierge, had
died during the night, we raised enough
money to buy a coffin; but chancing to
look from my window later on, I saw her
borne away on a board, with a few paper
flowers strewn over her and four common
candles casting a sickly glare and much
grease over the waxen figure. The father
carried the board on his head, and many
times stopped to gossip and laugh as he
passed away down the street toward the
shrine of Guadalupe, there to cast her in a
rough pit, and returning, hold high revel

with his friends on the money we have given for the coffin. Undoubtedly, as we pass out to-night, he will shower blessings on our heads, not for what we have wished to do for the dead—he could never be made to understand that—but for the opportunity we have afforded him for getting drunk on pulque. But let us follow to Guadalupe. Out one of the broad avenues of the city he passes with his strange, sad burden; now in the deep shadow of some old church, where the semi-darkness causes the candles to faintly illuminate the dead; now in the broad glare of brilliant sunlight, showing up the tawdry decorations and robbing even death of its majesty; again he pauses for half an hour before a pulque shop, while he drinks and chatters, his burden on a chair beside him, and toward it neither he nor the dozens near him glance, even for a moment. Meanwhile there has slowly approached through the crowd an old shaggy dog, which now sits on its haunches by the rude bier and closely regards the dead. As we draw near, he raises his eyes to ours, full of sadness, and I should say, if a dog could weep, full of tears. He remembers his frolics through the sunshine and shadows, and many a night's sleep with his head pillowed on the little form so silent before him now, and he is the only one who, remembering, regrets. The queer procession starts again ere long. The man by this time has an ill-smelling cigar between his teeth and so much pulque down his throat that his movements are unsteady, and I dread lest the burden on his head be cast into the gutter. The dog follows, and the stream of human life flows on past them, thinking little, caring less. Now a woman with a tray of greasy tortillas brushes by him; now he is rudely ordered to halt, while a gay cavalcade of horsemen gallops past. At last, leaving the street of the town, he joins in the vast crowd of pilgrims, all journeying toward the sacred shrine of Guadalupe, sacred since the Virgin showed herself there to Indian John. About three miles from the city, on one of the foot hills of the mountains, stands the cathedral, marking the spot, and behind and above it mounts the city of the dead, with its fantastic monuments. The church itself is cathedral in size and richness, and is full of votive offerings like that of Notre Dame de la Garde at Marseilles. Here at all seasons of the year, like as unto Benares, come thousands on thousands of the people, and here they kneel in silent ranks, hours at a time. In the city of the dead rich tombs and monuments mark the sleeping places of the wealthy—long rows of unmarked graves—those where the poor are

cast in uncoffined. Near one of these the
man has paused, and placing his burden on
the ground, bends for a moment in—let us
hope, if not prayer, at least remembrance.
Then he departs swiftly, while the old dog
comes slowly forward and lies down beside
the dead. The afternoon shadows grow
longer and longer ; still he lies there. His
mournful eyes gaze outward past the shrine
and its countless worshipers ; past the long
dusty highway, down which was so lately
borne his dead companion ; past the city
and her lakes and the groves of the Alameda, where he has played with the child
in her short life-time, to the point where the
setting sun has turned the snowy cones of
the great mountains into gold. Amidst all
that glory is he looking for the spirit of his
dead playmate ? The silent form before
him seems almost touched into life by the

THE SHRINE OF GUADALUPE.

benediction of departing day. Then the
night falls suddenly.

As we return homeward, sounds of bois-
terous merriment greet our ears, and we see
through the portals of the house a group of
people across whose faces the flickering light
of a fire casts grotesque shadows. Amongst
them is the father of the dead child. With his
companions he holds high carnival, because
the Virgin has taken her unto herself. So
he untwists the end of the well-filled pulque
skin, which is enthroned on a table beside
him, and allows each in turn to take long
draughts of the nauseous liquid, after every
one of which their faces become more and
more besotted in expression. To such use
is being put the money that we gave for her
coffin.

CHAPTER XXXIV.

I REMEMBER being one day in the cemetery at Havana—not the Camp Santo, but the new cemetery out near the Governor General's Palace, when up drove an elegant hearse, followed by a victoria, in which, behind liveried servants, sat two young men. After some service in the mortuary chapel the coffin was borne into the cemetery and we followed to see what would happen. Passing the portion set off for the rich, which was full of elegant monuments, they approached a long row of empty and newly-filled graves. One of the men taking a ticket from his pocket handed it to the grave diggers—two most repulsive-looking negroes. They nodded and pointed

to the nearest empty pit. Lifting off the
coffin lid there was exposed to view the form
of a young woman beautifully dressed, her
features covered by a lace veil. With scant
ceremony the diggers seized the body by
the head and feet and literally dropped it
into the open grave, which not being long
enough almost doubled it up. Then in-
verting the coffin, they struck it a few
blows on the bottom, as one does to
empty a basket. One dropped a coarse
blanket into the grave and then the stone
and rocks were shoveled on, while the
elegantly dressed young men carefully
wiping the dust from the coffin, returned
it to the hearse and drove off in their
own perfectly appointed carriage. Graves
there cost $60.00—" useless expense—when
you are dead you are dead and will not
know whether you are coffined or not—so
why waste money?"

CHAPTER XXXV.

A S you gaze out over this busy city, surrounded by its wondrously beautiful valley and mountains, your thoughts must turn in retrospection over the centuries that have passed, and in their passage brought her such hours of distress and triumph. You will realize that, as the great waves of time and change have rolled over Mexico, those from the northward have brought her prosperity, while those from the south and east, little but sorrow and distress. Do you laugh at such an assertion? If so I think a deeper study of the history of Mexico will cause you to change your mind. From the northward in the forgotten ages came the Toltecs, savages, it is true, yet they brought with them many of the arts of the present day, gathered the people together in towns and cities, and taught them a measure of government. To that race we trace all the wonderful carvings to be found throughout the land from Texas to Panama. They were heathens and cannibals, but never the latter in the usual acceptation of that term. Cannibalism with them being a religious function, only those sacrificed to their gods were so consumed; and if such a term may be here used, it was done decently and in order—as it were—a sort of Holy Communion. I do not uphold the practice even in heathens, but to me it is not so horrible as the awful tortures of the Inquisition. Indeed, there was rarely any torture about it, and it was a fate welcomed by many as a sure passport to their realms of bliss—

while the Inquisition, not content with
torturing the body, condemned the soul
to eternal damnation. After the Toltecs
came the Aztecs, still a race of savages,
but very different savages from those we
found in our northern land. Cortez discovered them living in well-ordered towns
and comparatively well governed, especially was this the case in the great city
of Cholula where now the lonely pyramid
looks down on a few wretched huts and
miserable people. What possible good
followed in his train? A small upper
class may have become more civilized and
enlightened, but the masses are to my
mind but little better off now than in
the days when the heathen gods claimed
thousands for their altars. You may say that
Cortez brought the true cross, introduced
the religion of Jesus. Granted, and had
it rested there, or been carried on in

the manner ordained by the Nazarene,
Mexico would to-day be three hundred
years in advance of her present condition, and the nations to the north and
south of the Rio Grande would become
one with no delay; but it was not to be.
The shadow of Torquemada spread rap-
idly over this unhappy land, cursing place
and people, and it was not until 1815
that the Inquisition was formally banished
from the land, declared a dead institution.

CHAPTER XXXVI.

HOW different would have been the fate of this city and this land had Cortez, after suppressing the sacrifices, suppressed also the advocates of the Inquisition. Of course he would have been burned for his good intentions, and like Napoleon his ambition was centered in himself. He had little love for Church or State, save when they tended to his own advancement. He was followed by a long line of regents, emperors and presidents of the same pattern, until we come to the present incumbent, Porfirio Diaz, who really seems to have the welfare of the land at heart. Enter the palace below us there and gaze on their

portraits—read their histories. Even in
our day, what were Hidalgo, Santa Anna,
Iturbide and Juarez? Surely, each and all
of them, men who loved Mexico some,
but themselves infinitely more; and, therefore, used their unfortunate country as a
means whereby to gratify their own pleas-
ures, and further their own personal glory.
Maximilian would have done good to all,
but he was not allowed even to try it. We
have had some curses in our land—such
as the burning of the witches and slavery.
The former was wiped out very quickly
and left no evil effects. The latter, while
terrible in its results to the South, only
affected a small portion of our land, while
we, being at all times alive to the awful
character of the ulcer, were, therefore, on
guard against it, and when the time came
cut it out. Had it gone on, in the end
its shadow would have equaled that of

the Inquisition over Mexico; but, thank
God, those shadows have vanished from
both peoples. As I leaned over the para-
pet, taking my farewell view of the ancient city, the cracked bells of Santa
Domingo sent up a jangling, useless remonstrance against the destruction of its
order. The sounds of life were many,
and echoed and re-echoed against the
towers of the great cathedral opposite.
Purple shadows gathered around Chapultepec and over lakes and mountains.
Toward Guadalupe thousands of pilgrims
were moving, there to remain all night,
and so be in time for the morrow's feast
of the Virgin. Suddenly the golden light
of the day went out as though a gust
of wind had extinguished a great illumi-
nation. Again, Popocatapetl and Ixtaccihuatl gleamed for an instant as a parting
unto us; again, the snowy form of the

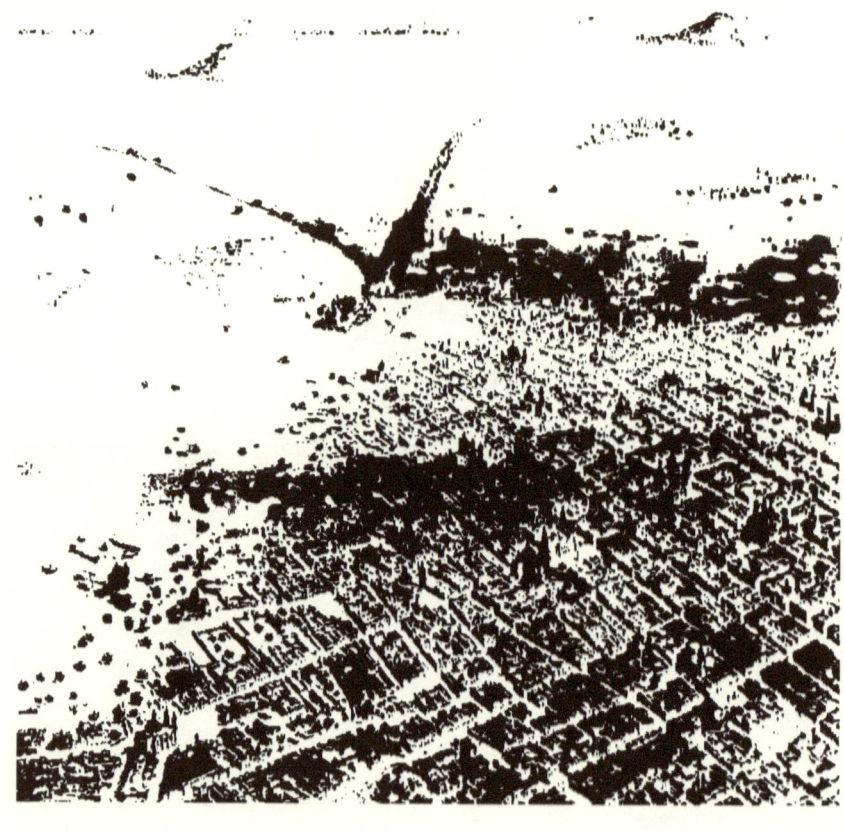

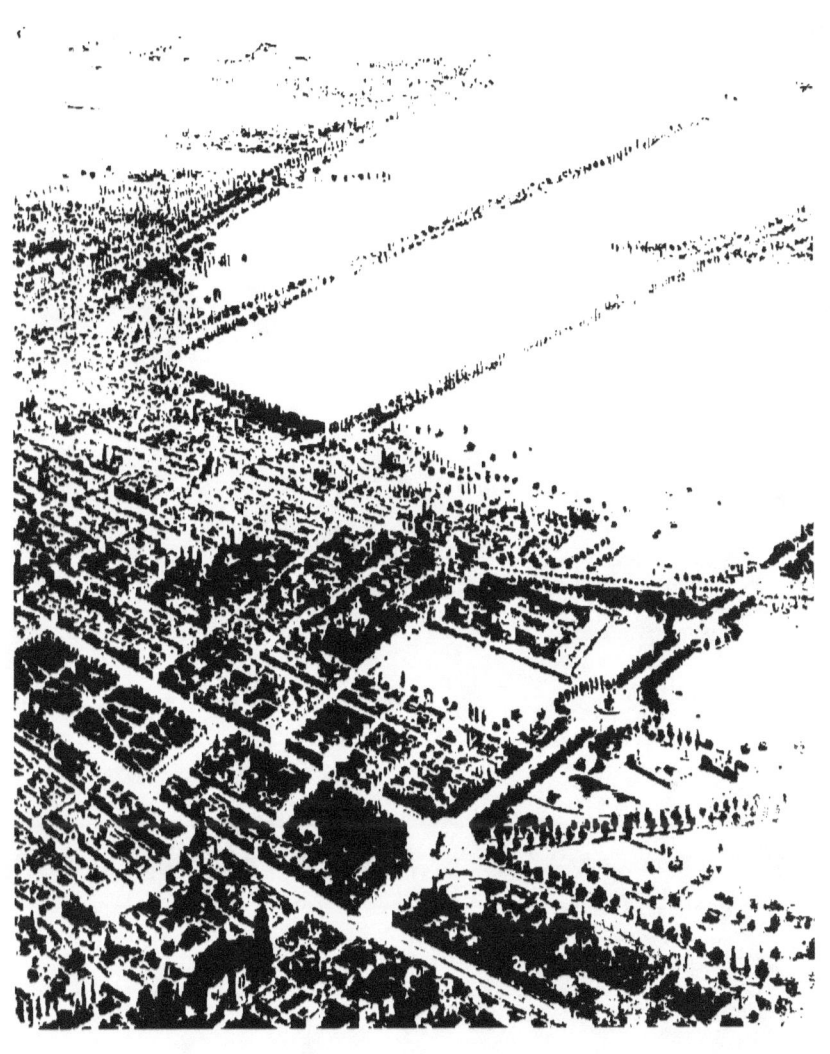

"white woman" blazed forth as though in a golden chamber, then all vanished into darkness—while from the world below, our ears were saluted by a wild, shrill whistle telling of the trains incoming from the north, bringing more and more and more each day, month and year the millions of a peaceful conquest, over whose reign, let us hope, the superstitions of the past can cast no shadow.

CHAPTER XXXVII.

ALL that is very well from the standpoint of progress, etc.; but from that
of the dreamer and traveler I feel very
much as I once heard a lady say as she
gazed from Sparrow Hill on the oriental
splendors of Moscow, " Well, I trust all this
will soon pass away, but I am glad I have
seen it before it was disturbed." So it was
with Mexico. One is happy to have seen
her picturesqueness before the influence of
the north has changed it all, thereby reduc-
ing it to the utterly uninteresting and com-
mon-place characteristics of our own cities,
each and all of them better places in which
to live, but certainly possessing very little
beauty. So if these notes should induce

any one to leave home for a few weeks and journey south to the old city, I shall be amply repaid for the writing thereof, and the traveler for having read them and followed in my footsteps, for on this same continent he will find a country containing people, towns, and cities almost as interesting as old Spain, and holding scenery far superior to any she can show. In fact, I rank it second only to the Himalayas. As regards the journey, if you do not suffer with sea-sickness, I should advise an entrance at Vera Cruz, thereby saving many miles of useless railway journey. You will have enough, at very least; but if you must come by rail, there are several new lines in from Texas. From the City of Mexico you should go seaward as far as Orizaba, that ride being one of the grandest on the globe. When you finally start northward, you will leave via El Paso, or over Eagle Pass, as your destination will decide. Mexico is changing, it is true, but it will be several generations before she ceases to be of interest. I love personal liberty too much ever to travel on a set plan; but for those who feel otherwise, those parties of " Raymond" offer a reasonable and most comfortable method of seeing Mexico. Traveling with their own train complete, they move when and how they please, and for ladies who must go alone, or not at all, offer excellent opportunities for so doing. I have watched many of them, and I know that the attention and service is excellent. Not knowing any of the managers of the said company—in fact, never having even seen them—I am getting nothing for this advertisement, and only offer it for the benefit of those who wish strange countries for to see, and yet hesitate to go because they have none to go with them. I think, on trying it, they will find that they receive the best of care, from the moment they enter on the tour until it is over—all save the memories, which can never be "over," which will be a joy forever.

CHAPTER XXXVIII.

WE are having a picnic to-day—it being the 22nd of February. In one of the Tivoli Gardens, outside the city, all the Americans, English and society people of the town have gathered. At the banquet our minister makes all the necessary and proper remarks about the father of his country, and is answered by a Spaniard in the language of old Castile. We are assured this "answer" is all that it should be, but it might be the Book of Genesis or the ten commandments for all we know or care. Being short of champagne glasses, I am drinking out of the gourd of a "Granadilla," and am not sorry, as it holds much

more. However, soon the entrancing music
of the Danza brings all to their feet, and
we glide through the mazes of that most
fascinating dance. As its strains die away
we turn from one more day of pleasure
in this city of the south, and it is our
last, for to-morrow the train will bear us
northward, toward enlightenment and progress, toward the rush and roar and un-
rest of our own dear land. Dear? Yes,
most certainly, for we would not live elsewhere, would not hold allegiance to any
other banner than our starry one; but I
must acknowledge that the happiest, the
most complete days, months and years of
my life have been passed in foreign lands.
You say that ours will "possess all that
the rest of the world does in a thousand
years." Perhaps so; but we will not be
here to enjoy it, and I doubt whether
the view from the battlements of Heaven

will be either interesting or profitable, so I maintain that from a traveler's standpoint, after having once seen our country, there is little to tempt one to cover its vast reaches again. Other lands possess as grand and grander scenery, while the voyager has within easy reach all the inexhaustible resources of art and music, of history and antiquity. He need never waste a moment of his time, nor wear his life out in weary, hot journeys. Those who have suffered in the crossing of our continent in summer will fully understand what I mean.

There is one of these railway journeys before us now. It will take us three nights and two days to reach El Paso, though but 1100 miles away. However, one is never in a hurry in the south.

CHAPTER XXXIX.

THE eating houses on the Mexican Central are at this time (1889) something
fearful. So we lay in a stock of provisions
to last until the Rio Grande is passed. The
train for the north is crowded, and our car
contains the interesting and uninteresting
lot usually to be found in traveling. In the
drawing-room an English party has settled
itself—two or three bright-faced girls and
an elderly man, evidently the father; his
only objection to the journey being the de-
privation of his "morning tub." They are
pleasant people, and one enjoys talking to
them. En route to India, they look forward
with great anticipations to California, the
Yosemite, etc. One can easily see that

the combined wonders of the world, natural and otherwise, would scarce fulfill
these anticipations. The center of the car
is occupied by a minister, his wife, and
four of the worst children it has ever
been my misfortune to meet with. The
wife, a pale, little, worn-out women, ex-
pends all her energies in keeping them from
"torturing father," who sits alone in his section, deeply engaged in the composition of
sermons which shall astonish the world and
hand his name down to posterity; that said
world does not already worship at his shrine
is evidently the " fault of its own blindness."
Thin to cadaverousness, dressed in orthodox
black, his sunken eyes expressing all that
intense egotism so common to his order—all
the utter intoleration of those who dare to ·
differ with him—writing, writing, and mut-
tering to himself, while ever and anon his
claw-like hands wave in gesticulation as he

addresses some vast, imaginary audience. Utterly absorbed in self, he never turns thought or glance toward the assistance of his poor worn-out wife, though she appears almost ready to faint in her battle with their children. She never raises her voice in remonstrance, for "Have ye not heard the words of Paul, 'Oh let the women keep silence, all.'" And silent she will be until the greater silence comes down upon her— until the greater rest with its "peace, be still" spreads its mantle of quiet over weary heart and brain. There are heroines whose names are never written save on God's roll of honor. There are also men who would still burn witches with delight if they dared to do so.

CHAPTER XL.

EN ROUTE.

WE do not leave the train at Queretaro. There is nothing of interest
there save the hill upon which Maximilian
was murdered, and that we see from the
train. At Aguas Calientes the people are
bathing in thousands in the naturally warm
water as it flows through the ditches. It is
the first time I have seen them show the
slightest disposition to approach water of
any sort. How wretched and degraded
they appear as they squat in long rows on
the banks or paddle around in the stream,
and how do they ever manage to get back
into those heaps of vermin-ladened rags
that lie around? They seem to be able to

live on nothing. If happy enough to possess a deformed child, who can be made to
beg, the entire family, retiring from work,
lives on the alms it receives, which must be
little enough, even now with every train
bringing hundreds of tourists into the land.
To give to all these beggars would impover-
ish a Rothschild. A group near, four most
wretched, evil-looking beings, is composed
of a perfectly healthy and most villainous-
looking man, a woman, and a grown son,
quite their equal in degradation, while the
bread winner is a wretchedly deformed little
girl, who stands with outstretched palms
before them. She seems to be blind,
though her splendid eyes are marred in
no way, and she also possesses every other
ill that flesh is heir to. One can not help
giving her something, though it is evident
she will profit nothing while surrounded by
such harpies. In all the thousand miles

between the capital and the Rio Grande, the way is almost lined with such sights. There are millions of these wretches, so I would beg of those who favor our annexation of Mexico to come down and see for themselves before this step is taken; then perhaps they may pause and ask, "What will we do with these?" The land is so incrusted with poverty, vice, and wretchedness, that a hundred Niagaras must be turned over it before any sane man would care to annex such an ulcer. The same holds true of Cuba. A grand climate, a rich and beautiful island, a vile people, possessing all the degradation and disease that man has ever heard of.

CHAPTER XLI.

ZACATECAS.

THIS is the highest point in Mexico; over 8,000 feet. We feel this altitude and the desire to get away is almost unbearable. Nor is it lessened by the kindly advice of a native who sits at breakfast with us. The hotel is an abandoned monastery, dark and cold. Cold— so penetrating that it seems to chill ones life blood—creeps down the spine with the hand of death. The sun pours brilliantly down and over all; but it is a cruel kind of light that holds neither life nor warmth. Seated at breakfast in the semi-gloom of the old refectory we are entertained by said native, who enlarges

with apparent glee upon the "generally
fatal effects of the climate here upon
foreigners." He tells us that we may
feel apparently well and yet be on the
verge of a collapse—that it always strikes
suddenly and in the shape of a chill down
the spine. (We have each and all had
chills down the spine ever since we entered the town.) We look at one another
with silent requests to "break it gently
to those at home and not to bother about
taking the body back." Two of us rush
off in wild agony, and after seizing a
donkey and mounting into the panniers,
which hang on either side of his shaggy
body, insist upon a visit to the church
whose cross gleams high above us. The
only one left behind appears on a balcony over our heads, and suggests that if
the present altitude has scared us into
fits that of the church will surely finish

matters—all of which has no effect, and we start off. The lady of the ride is somewhat heavy while I am light, so the donkey is now and then disconcerted by finding one pannier between his legs while the other has mounted his back. My view is from the latter point superb, while her power of locomotion in the former position materially assists the donkey in the ascent. I think the beast selects every rock of any size and insists upon crossing it with the intention, I fancy, of scraping off his "steerage passenger." He does not mind me in the least, and in fact, I fancy, thinks me, as has often been the case, somewhat ornamental. Ever and anon he pauses over some immense chasm and wildly shakes himself. At such moments I can see a pair of "walking shoes" describing geometrics, angles and circles beneath me, but the

owner thereof, being of a pugnacious disposition, holds on tightly, and in such form
we are finally deposited before the shrine
of the Virgin. I doubt if that saintly per-
sonage ever had pilgrims arrive in like
fashion before.

The view is grand but very barren.
Vast stretches of arid plains with encircling chains of purple mountains; little
or no vegetation of any sort—all seems
lurid and desolate. So we hasten downward, deserting the donkey for the more
comfortable, if not surer, method of walking—constant practice enabling him to get
his four legs down the rocks better and
faster than we can our four. In order,
therefore, not to undergo the ignominy of
walking into town, I secure the beast, upon
which we finally mount again, not as before in the panniers, but far back—near his

tail—to which, I am ashamed to say, we
do not hesitate, when necessity requires,
to cling wildly. As we pass downward we come suddenly upon a drove of
wretched, dirty men, scarcely clad at all,
and driven along like swine. They are
prisoners returning from their day's work.
There can certainly be no after punish-
ment for wretches like these. Hell itself
can show no more ghastly-looking faces than
theirs as they stumble along. Their bare
shoulders receive blow after blow from the
keepers, who would not treat their beasts
as they treat these men, "made in the
image of the Creator." Nearing the
prison each and all are searched as they
pass within, in order to see that they have
stolen none of the precious metal over
which they have labored like dogs. What
could they do with it? It would be
seized at once and all they would get

would be added blows. A man had much
better be dead than cast into a Mexican
prison. He rarely comes out alive, and
an order of transportation from one prison
to another means "death on the way."
The cruelties in these places are only
equaled in Turkey or Persia.

It is hard to feel that you are absolutely helpless to offer any aid or comfort
to so much misery; but even as we look
the keeper turns on us with a snarl like
a wolf, and I doubt not we would scarcely
fancy what is said could we understand it.

Our dreams at night are cursed by
visions of all this wretchedness, inter-
mingled with sudden attacks on our own
health by ghastly, skeleton-like figures,
named fever and chills. So it is with
no regret that we start for the station

the following morning. As we do not stop at Chihuahua, this is our last point in Old Mexico. We do not get off without one more example of man's cruelty— not to fellowmen this time, but to dumb beasts. The great silver mines of the Rothschilds are here, and when the ore is gotten out and well covered with chemicals they turn old broken down animals thereon to tramp out the metal. The chemicals in the end eat away their hoofs and the poor beasts are turned into the desert to starve.

As you travel from end to end of this land so richly endowed by the hand of a bounteous nature or a great Creator, you are constantly struck with its inexhaustible resources, and dream often of what its future under an honest rule and different religion might be. The moment

we leave the Terra Calientes, which, so
far as I can judge, produce magnificent
crops of yellow fever on their barren
sands—that and nothing but that—and
enter the provinces of Cordova and Orizaba—we have around us vast sugar
and coffee plantations, equal, if not superior, to those of Cuba, and a climate
unsurpassed in all the world. Here alone
an immense population could be supported
where is now but sparse settlements. The
water powers are fine, the fruits are de-
licious, the flowers beautiful. The air at
Orizaba is like wine, and one could almost
desire to live on there forever. Passing
upward to the great tableland you may
travel for fifteen hundred miles to the
northward and a thousand miles to the
southward and be at all times within
sight of mountains, beautiful to look upon,
and rich with untold and inexhastible

wealth—filling the soul of the painter
with deep satisfaction that they are so
beautiful and with envy that his brush
can do that beauty no justice; while
to him who searches for the treasures
of these hills dreams equal to Aladdin's
may be fulfilled. There are enough of
riches here to run the world, and there
is misery and poverty enough around one
to damn those who are the cause thereof
forever. The government of Mexico is
struggling hard and with much success
to counteract the effect of three hundred
years of misrule, by a power that has
not yet thrown up the game. That the
victory must in the end perch on the
banners of freedom, progress and justice
none can doubt—this being the 19th and
not the 16th century. All along the route
to the north from the capital, hordes of
miners throng each station, and a more

terrible looking lot it would be hard to find—clothed in tattered and filthy sacking, flesh scarred, seamed and calloused with eternal exposure to violent changes of temperature, faces sodden by a lifetime of hunger, hard work and wretchedness. They look more animal than human, and their lack-luster eyes gaze upon the traveler from another land with absolutely no expression ; nor can he bring a gleam of light into their faces unless he shows a little money. Then the swift, lurking, stealthy side glance of these half savages convinces him that it is well the sun shines and he is not alone with them. Aside from that glance they pay no attention to one who is so far apart from their lives that he can have absolutely nothing in common with them. If they could rob him —well and good. They would thank the blessed Virgin for the privilege. As they

can not, he may go his way. I doubt
if they could be convinced that their
condition could be bettered. Look at that
lot yonder—thirty or more—just in from
some mine in the distant mountains, fifty
miles away. Are they human? All down
in· the dirt of the road together, like so
many swine, most of them asleep. They
will be driven back shortly, only to come
again with ore for those who already
have millions. How different from the
hardy, healthy faces we meet with amongst
our mining population, where clear eyes and
cheerful voices greet us so pleasantly. And
yet we as a nation are, in the estimation of
these poor wretches, "heretics, and therefore damned;" whilst they have lived for
centuries under the benign and enlighten-
ing influences of "Holy Church!" If I
have spoken too strongly about that same
"Holy Church," it is for the very reason

that I know how grand she can be and could have been; so I find less excuse for her, in that by her intoleration of all other sects, and by her inquisition, she has kept poor Mexico and many other lands and peoples so long in the blackness of midnight!

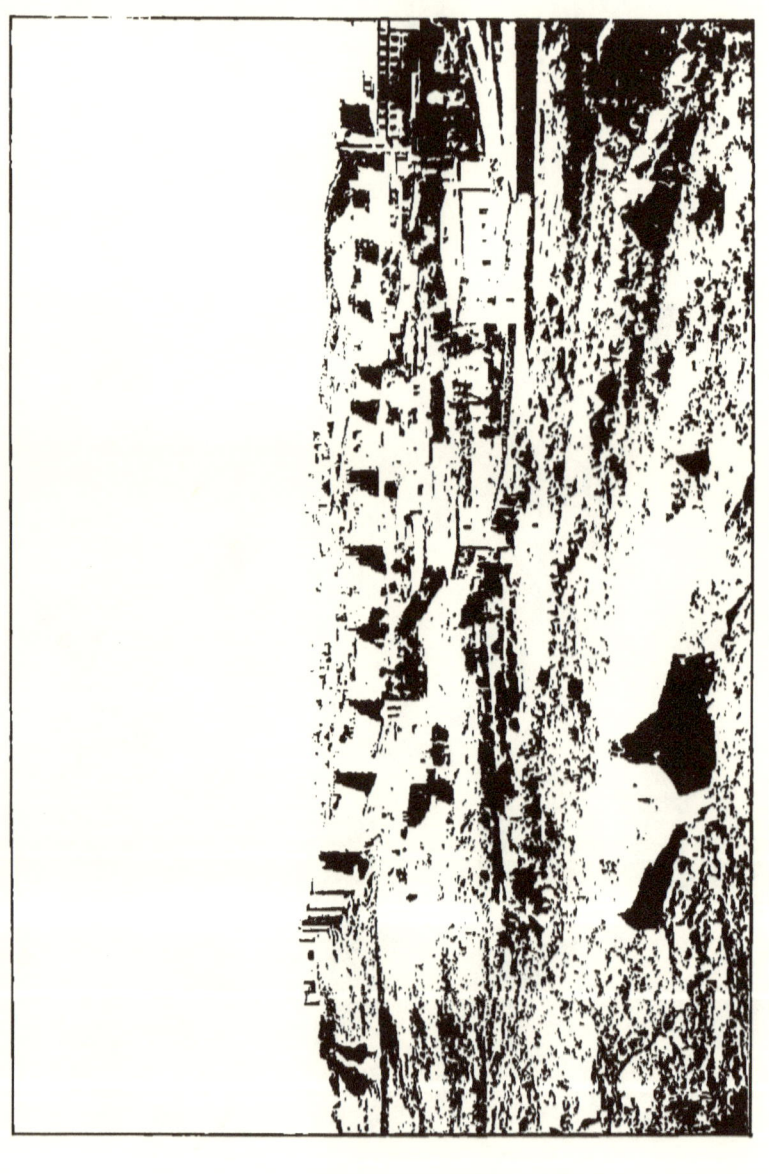

AVILA, THE BURIAL-PLACE OF TORQUEMADA.

CHAPTER XLII.

O NE bright, sunny day in old Spain, I passed in rambling with my guide, one Leonard by name—if you go to Madrid, ask for him—over the ancient city of Avila; it stands on the barren plains of the province of that name to the north of the capital, and is a perfect specimen of a feudal city. Great walls, broken in many places by high towers, encircle the narrow, shady streets, where I paused, ever and anon, to gaze up at some richly carved portal—telling of the grandeur, now long since passed away—or stood in the shadow of some doorway as a procession, in the still unforgotten glory of the middle ages, wound its way from the great cathedral to some church or shrine beyond the walls. There were crosses of gold held high in air, which caught the gleam of the sun and flashed bright spots of light over the dark walls of the old palaces. Black-robed priests and white-robed acolytes, bearing painted banners and shaking out clouds of incense, followed reverently the holy symbols. At the head of all walked one holding high aloft the "blessed sacrament." Then I knew that some soul was passing to its maker—that the priests of the "Holy Church" were on their way to administer her last rites. As they moved along the people knelt in reverence, and the noise and bustle of the old town sank into silence. Following in their wake I passed under one of the great gates, its loopholes frowning, its portcullis still in place, out onto the desolate plains beyond, which

stretched away in all directions, barren
and treeless, with nothing to break their
dead level save long lines of stone walls,
flat-roofed villages or ruined towers. The
" procession of the dying" turned to the
right, but my guide kept straight onward
down the dusty highway, until finally in
the shaded court of an old monastery I
found myself gazing upon an unpreten-
tious tomb, while at the name inscribed
thereon, "Torquemada," I started as
though a cobra had suddenly reared its
head. Here then rested—if his body can
ever rest—he who has cursed so many
millions and been the direct cause of the
downfall of so many nations ; for, just so
certainly as they, listening to his teach-
ings, followed them, their day of glory and
progress passed away. Look at Spain in
1492. Ferdinand and Isabella had at last
conquered the Moors, and soon the land

would have been rid of the Infidels. All the future was golden with glorious promise, when into the royal tent at Grenada crept the black-robed figure of a monk —and from that hour the glory of Spain steadily but surely declined. Look at the panorama of decay as it slowly unrolls itself athwart the pages of the centuries. See the greatness and the glitter of the armies of the nation as they pass under the "Puerto del Sol" and enter the court of the myrtles; how triumphant and full of promise sounds the music of the many trumpets. Long is the reign of Ferdinand and Isabella, but even upon it the smirches of decay appear. Then comes the reign of crazy Joan and Philip the Handsome. The realm is priest-ridden. Where in the days of the Moors all the arts and sciences prevailed, now is sloth and silence and decay, while the *auto da fè* blackens the

land with its cinders. Charles the Fifth
meets with defeat in the lowlands and
abdicates his crown from very weariness.
Then an evil face, thin and ghastly, with
narrow forehead and sinister eyes, sur-
mounting a crooked figure—clothed in
rusty black, comes stalking by, and you
know you are in the presence of the
terrible Philip. He has lost his German
Empire—Mary of England is dead, and the
Armada scattered. He has murdered his
innocent son and heir, Don Carlos, but
he has builded the Escorial to the memory
of Holy St. Lawrence, which act of piety
his priests assure him will surely save his
soul, if he will offer up the souls and
bodies of the countless heretics, which so
infest the land, and which even the terrors
of the Inquisition can not conquer. There
is a picture in Madrid which shows him so

engaged—it is a terrible thing. Now the
scene changes to those small, dark rooms
just off the high altar in the Escorial.
The great church glitters with gold and
precious stones. Over all, the light of
thousands of candles sheds its mellow
rays; but nothing can bring light or hope
to the mind of the dying king. Here,
where he has "ruled the world with three
inches of paper," he is paying his debt to
nature and an outraged God, and here he
passes away, tortured with fear and doubt,
shuddering at his past, with no hope as
to his future, and all through the work
started by the monk, who sleeps so
quietly in the old convent at Avila. To-
day Spain is just starting onward once
more; for, as she suffered the most, so
she is the last to recover. So it was in
France, in Germany, in Italy, in Mexico.
In fact, wherever the Inquisition held

PHILLIPE II at an *auto da fé.*

sway, and not until her yoke was broken forever did the angel of peace and progress turn its face toward them. Look at the difference in England and our own land where the Inquisition never obtained a footing. The tortures in England were fearful, but the Inquisition never obtained a footing there. As I stood by Torquemada's grave that day, in Avila, I horrified a Frenchman by the assertion that this monk had influenced to a much greater degree than Napoleon the history and the peoples of the world. The latter was a great general, but, like all whose ambition is centered in and for themselves, his work was not far reaching nor enduring; and I can not see that the world is any better or worse for his having lived. But Torquemada has stretched his skeleton hands until their shadow has covered most of the known world, and lasted undiminished through centuries, changing the fate of nations, almost altering the face of nature—cursing ever and always. And what, I wonder, was his greeting when he came face to face with Him whose message to saint and sinner was "Peace be unto you?"

CHAPTER XLIII.

STILL, when you consider the vast good done by the Church of Rome, you are ready to forgive much in it that is bad. No other denomination has sent forth such hosts of missionaries, such armies of nurses for the sick and dying, as that of Rome; and the good that has been done can not be estimated by the gold of the earth. So where a government, like ours or that of England, forces that church to confine herself to matters spiritual, great good and nothing but good is the result. It is only when she is possessed of temporal power that such abuses as have cursed Mexico have crept in. Opposed by the government the Inquisition itself could not have existed. Even now when it has long since given up the ghost, it has left a heritage of ignorant priesthood to curse these people. Mexico had more than a century the start of the north, yet where is she to-day in comparison? And who has cowed her people down, and kept them down, save a priesthood, knowing that an enlightenment of the masses meant an end to their power? Therefore they threw the weight of that power against poor Maximilian and Carlotta ranged on the side of progress. If there were any signs of such progress for the people in 1879, I failed to see it. The upper classes were rich and cultivated, but the middle and lower were like the masses in Sicily, but of a lower grade; for not even in that most degraded portion of Italy does one see thousands on thousands clothed

in nothing save wretched rags of coffee
sacking, while in some of the sugar
plantations they are not clothed at all.
Every vestige of thought and feeling
seems to have vanished long ago from
their faces, so that it is almost impossible as one looks at them to imagine
that they are human like ourselves. Is
it so, indeed? Are they men or animals?
Could they ever love any one or ever
long for the absent? Can their besotted,
brutish faces ever show gleams of reason?
Are they one whit more enlightened or
advanced than the Aztecs? Those were
cannibals, these are murderers and thieves.
Our own land holds none such; yet we
are on the same continent. Who then is
to blame?

CHAPTER XLIV.

CHIHUAHUA is passed at sunset, but with no desire on our part to stop over. As the morning breaks, looking from my window I see a great gulch at the bottom of which flows a sluggish stream, the Rio Grande, almost empty, as this is the dry season. We are still in Mexico, but across the gully with its willows and its mud, a wild-looking figure in leather clothing and broad-brimmed hat dashes shoutingly along. It is a cow-boy. That is our own dear land. The air seems to grow clearer and purer with the knowledge. We have reached the borders of a promised land, where each and all are as they make themselves.

The very vegetation of the earth seems changed. Gone are the cacti plants and the glistening magnolias, while vast masses of feathery chaparrál spread away like an ocean of delicate green, until their waves break at the base of Sierra Blanca, glowing pink in the morning light to the eastward. The distant air has that intensely clear, quivering appearance that one always associates with the wide freedom of our western plains, and seems full of life and health, not ladened with sickness and death, while the skies are of a bright, rain-washed cheerfulness. Over there, all is life, all is progress. While here around us, in this old town of Juarez, life and hope have long since passed away. Down her narrow, dusty streets you see the slumbering forms of her people in many doorways and corners. Will they ever awaken, or will they not rather slumber on and on until they gradually sink into and become part of the very earth itself; while above them, burying them deeper and deeper as the ages pass, sweeps the tide of a new life—the manners and customs of a new people? Then these will be forgotten utterly, or faintly remembered as some shadowy tradition of the long ago. Then will the curse of superstition be removed forever from our fair western continent. Then Mexico will be ours, heart and soul. Now, you might as well endeavor to mate the wild, free broncho of our northern plains with some skulking jackal of these yellow mountains, as to form a union between our people and these hordes to the southward.

CHAPTER XLV.

A S much as we have enjoyed the tour, it is with a feeling of intense relief that we leave the train at Juarez, and smilingly submit to the customs inspection. We would certainly not have grumbled at any tax placed upon us so long as it came from an American. It is strange that a narrow river can separate two such different peoples, wide apart as the poles in manners, with centuries between them as to customs, yet within rifle shot of each other. As we start across the stream, the town of Juarez is spread out around us, white, hot and silent. A few wretched dogs, skulking wolf-like along, a poor donkey, pulque ladened, whose owner gives us our last touch of Spanish in a cataract of oaths, as he showers blows upon the patient little beast. We are strongly tempted to get out, and, seizing the latter, turn him loose on the other side, where he can forever kick up his heels and roll in freedom with no end of "elbow room."

Yonder, into the gates of the prison pass some wretched beings, who shrink away as they near the brutal-looking keeper, knowing that his word means life or death to them; though I doubt not the latter would be preferred, were it to come quickly, to the lingering tortures of the former in a Mexican jail. A priest in greasy-black soutane and long, shovel-shaped hat, has just come from that house of mourning and now stands in close conversation with—surely —yes—

"RUMPLESTILTSKIN,"

a dwarf, saffron-colored, with evil eyes, dressed in rusty-black velveteen embroidered in much tawdry gilt and many beads. From his belt protrude the handles of three or four pistols and knives, while on his head a sombrero, gorgeous with cords and a feather and enormous in size, tilts over his leering, hypocritical face. With one last glance we pass onward, receiving a parting salute from the sentinel at the bridge as he murmurs "adios," and, landing on the other side, have our ears split asunder by a voice whose equal I have never heard. It comes from a mouth of gigantic proportions, behind which roll in a black face, two laughing eyes, "Grand Central Hotel! Dis way for de omnibus; plenty of time for dinner. I don car whar you's going." You have no notion unless you have taken such a tour what a relief that •nig-

ger was to us, for we had, without being fully conscious thereof, been upon a
constant strain of mind and body. I have
experienced the same feeling in Russia,
but never elsewhere.

Behind us all is asleep and has been
asleep these centuries, while El Paso is
a wide-awake, cow-boy town, with a boom
on, where one must move quickly or get
shot.

Having some hours to spare before
the trains separate our party, we spend
it in loafing around this western "city,"
gazing in at saloon doors and barber
shops with as much interest as we did
into the cathedral of the capital, and eating with great relish the tough steak and
soda biscuits of the hotel, washed down

by the vilest coffee imaginable; but every thing pleased.

Here we part, after many weeks of pure delight, all the ills forgotten, all the joys remembered. Some go to the westward, while I turn eastward toward the point where Sierra Blanca seems to block the way. As my train moves onward it approaches the river. "In the purple mists of evening" I see across its willows and sluggish current low, square houses, on whose flat roofs stand some figures with hands shading their eyes from the sunlight as they gaze intently westward, "toward the region of the sunset—toward the land of the hereafter"—watching, hoping and praying for the

"COMING OF MONTEZUMA."